DRESSED TO IMPRESS

An Erotica Collection

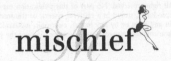

mischief

Mischief
An imprint of HarperCollins*Publishers*
77–85 Fulham Palace Road,
Hammersmith, London W6 8JB

www.mischiefbooks.com

A Paperback Original 2013

First published in Great Britain in ebook format by
HarperCollins*Publishers* 2012

A catalogue record for this book is
available from the British Library

ISBN-13: 9780007553440

Find out more about HarperCollins and the environment at
www.harpercollins.co.uk/green

CONTENTS

Differently
Catherine Paulssen

If getting tingly while watching your man shave made you eligible for a special club of women who could turn mundane rituals into the stuff of wicked daydreams, Debra would have been the club's founder. A woman likes her man well groomed, after all. For Debra, the act itself was its own reward. Could a man get any more Cary Grant than when he brushed some high-end shaving cream onto his cheeks and ran a razor over them, revealing his rugged jaw line, smooth and refreshed?

Through the open bathroom door Debra observed her husband, freshly out of the shower, a white terrycloth towel wrapped around his waist, drops of water trickling down the small of his back. She regarded him as he cupped his hands under the faucet and splashed his face with water. Now he reached for the brush, wetted it, then dipped it into the tub of fine English shaving cream she had given him for their last anniversary. He swirled the wet tips in the rich cream and soon his chiselled cheekbones had disappeared under a thick lather of opaque, herbal-scented mousse. She watched the play of his shoulder muscles as he swiped the brush up and down across his cheeks and neck. The hot damp air wafting from the bathroom carried a crisp, invigorating, slightly woody smell, making her mind wander back to the days when Nicholas's eyes would catch her own in the mirror, and he would turn around, hold out the shaving cream to her and ask if she'd help him. She remembered the cheeky grin on his face and how it felt to paint his strong jaw and neck with the frothy mousse while his hands played with her waistline. She remembered the silent innuendo between them as he moved the razor blade closely over his skin. When he was done, she would rub moisturiser onto his cheeks and chin, taking her time, and Nicholas's eyes would rest on her face the whole time until, finally, he would swoop her up in his arms, impatient to get her underneath him. His clean-shaven, cool cheeks would feel so fresh and alluring against her skin as he whispered sweet words into her ears ...

A sigh escaped her lips, and Nicholas turned. 'What's the matter, hm?' he asked, his voice soft.

She brushed the daydream away. 'Just – thinking.'

'And what are you thinking of?'

She searched his face. 'Us.'

He placed the badger brush away and raised his eyebrow. 'Us?'

Debra noticed a hint of tenderness in his voice – a small hint, to be sure, but a hint nonetheless. 'A different us.'

He paused for a moment, and his gaze turned towards the floor. Then, without a word, he picked up the razor and started to skim it along his face. Debra continued to watch him and, when he was done, got up to join him. She brushed his back as she moved beside him like a slender cat trying to show its affection, then reached for the aftershave lotion. 'Like me to massage your skin?'

He rinsed his face with cold water, put the razor away and dried his face. 'Debs, I need to get ready. Not now.'

'OK,' she whispered but didn't leave without pressing a tender kiss between his shoulder blades. At times like this, she usually felt like screaming at him. Not now, but when? When will you love me again like you used to?

Not today.

A high-pitched whimper called her to the children's room, and when Nicholas came down the stairs fifteen minutes later, dressed and ready to leave, she was trying to make Levi eat some of his mashed apricots while his brother Jake smeared her hair with mush-stained fingers.

Nicholas kissed both his sons quickly, careful to avoid a spoonful of fruit pulp aimed at his suit. 'Don't wait up for me. I'm meeting Al in the club after work.'

'Al?'

'Potential client.' He pressed a kiss on her cheek. 'It will be late.'

How she wished he would one time ask her to stay up! Wished she would one time see a silent question in his eyes: was it too much to ask of her not to go to bed, but to wait up for him?

Not today.

Today, she gave her husband a bright smile and wished him good luck at the meeting.

In the afternoon, she brought their two sons to visit her older sister, Rebecca.

'Hey, how are my favourite nephews?' Rebecca asked, ruffling Jake's hazelnut tuft as she removed him from the car seat.

'Happy to stay the night at Aunt Becky's, aren't you?' asked Debra as she lifted Levi, who was bubbling with excitement, and carried him into the house. They entertained the boys in their playpen for a while before returning to the car. Rebecca helped her sister take the stroller out of the trunk and eyed a pair of shiny black heels lying next to them.

'You're still determined to go there?' she asked.

'Uh huh.'

'Debbie, I don't know. That sort of nightclub …'

'It's just a place for good food and good drinks and first-rate entertainment!' said Debra, throwing her sister a reproachful look. 'I was there last week for training. Everyone was really nice and respectful. And anyways, it's just waitressing! No need to act as though I were becoming an escort or something.'

Rebecca pulled a pair of long, fingerless net gloves out of a bag. 'Just waitressing,' she said, raising an eyebrow. 'You'll show up at Nicholas's club dressed like Hugh Hefner's idea of a French maid!'

Debra shouldered the babies' diaper bags and yanked the gloves out of her sister's hands. 'How often do you and Dave have sex?'

Rebecca gave an amused frown. 'Don't know. Often enough, I guess.'

'So you'd say you're happy with your love life?'

'Pretty much, yes.'

Debra shut the trunk with a loud bang. 'Well, I'm not. And I doubt Nicholas is.' She straightened up. 'First, when we were trying to get pregnant, sex became this awkward mess. You know – we planned, we fretted, we followed rules and got all technical about it. And ever since the twins –' she continued, following her sister back inside the house '– we're always too tired and, well, I'm frustrated! I'm frustrated and I'm afraid ...' She took a deep breath.

'You're afraid of what?' Rebecca asked, closing the door behind them.

Debra sighed. 'That we lost it. You know – the spark.'

She looked at her older sister as if she held the cure to her worries. 'What if we killed it with all the fertility treatments and scheduled sex?'

Rebecca tilted her head. 'You're both just working too hard. And two toddlers – I don't know a *single* couple that doesn't complain about a slump after having kids.'

'They're fifteen months old, Becky!' Debra raised her voice to be heard over Jake's howling and reached for a stuffed ladybird he had thrown out of the playpen. 'Here, sweetie,' she said. Then, turning back to her sister: 'I can't even remember the last time we were relaxed and having fun and just – making love. Not performing or fulfilling some marital duty or …'

'Why don't you, I don't know, buy some lingerie? Book a spa together. Or you could –'

'And what else does *Cosmo* suggest?' Debra rolled her eyes. 'No. Me waitressing – that's how we met. And I want Nicholas to remember that I'm still that woman.'

'You didn't wear a black corsage at Ol' Flannery's Pub.'

'Well, that's the point, if you catch my drift.' Debra grinned mischievously. She turned to the boys. 'Be good, OK?' She pressed a kiss on both her sons' cheeks. 'Don't give Aunt Becky a hard time. Mummy will be back tomorrow. I love you lots and lots!' She gave Rebecca a hug. 'I owe you.'

Rebecca smiled patiently. 'Good luck, you crazy woman.'

'Thanks.' With a last look at the twins, Debra left her sister's house.

A few hours later, she entered the sophisticated lounge of the Connor's Club. The whole interior was a hymn of understated masculinity, inspired by Playboy clubs from the 1960s. Firm white leather chairs alternated with dark, glossy ones, their high backrests vanishing in the diffuse glow emitted by discreet table lights. Folding screens made of wengé wood divided the room into separate entities. Across from the entrance, set against a wall covered in mirrors, a bar shone under a cold silvery light.

Waitresses at Connor's wore dressy black corset leotards, tightly laced at the front, with matching net stockings and black patent-leather heels. Debra wasn't heavily made up, but false lashes and a bobbed wig à la Uma Thurman's *Pulp Fiction* look made her feel like a whole different person whenever she caught a glimpse of herself in the mirrors behind the bar.

Nicholas hadn't yet arrived, and she was as excited as she had been back at age 24 in Ol' Flannery's Pub, waiting for him to show up with his crowd of college friends every Thursday night, the highlight of her week.

She was waiting for the barman to fill the glasses for her latest order when she saw her husband's face reflected between the bottles of liquor staged along the wall. He was accompanied by Al, a red-cheeked, stocky man who must have been a good head shorter. Debra quickly placed the cocktails on her tray and hurried to the guests waiting for them in the far corner of the room. For the next half hour, she made sure not to come too close to Nicholas's table and tried her best not to ever look in his direction.

'Honey, can you cover for me?' Another waitress brushed Debra's arm as she headed out the back door for a cigarette. 'Just a few minutes?'

'Sure.' Debra exhaled. No more excuses. She was about to take an order from a group close to Nicholas's table when she heard a gravelly voice behind her. 'That's one fine piece of ass!'

A glance into the mirror told her that Nicholas's client was brazenly gorging on her behind. 'Wouldn't you agree?' Al asked, nudging her husband. Nicholas nodded and smiled politely.

'Oh, come on!' Al let out a puffy laugh. 'That's all?'

Nicholas shrugged. 'I'm a married man.'

It wasn't so much his words that made Debra glow inside, but the way he had said them. She had not heard the slightest trace of regret or weariness in his voice. In fact, he had sounded rather proud. She turned around and beamed at him. Nicholas caught her eyes and, for a split second, he smiled back. Then his eyes grew wide. His gaze wandered over her attire, thunderstruck, and Debra's hands grew damp.

'Can I get you anything?' she asked, quickly turning her eyes to Al.

'We'll have two Gibson Martinis.'

'Of course, sir.'

'Al, would you excuse me for a second?' she heard Nicholas say as she made her way to the bar. Next thing she knew, she was being dragged into a hallway that led to the smoking terrace.

'What the hell are you doing?' he hissed. The anger in his voice was not exactly the kind of agitation she'd hoped to spark.

'I – I wanted to surprise you,' she said, hanging her head. Not the great line she'd rehearsed when picturing this scene the past few weeks.

Nicholas huffed. 'Well, this *is* a surprise,' he said, his eyes bearing into her. 'So what – behind my back, you're entertaining random old men?'

'No! No. This is the first time!' She looked at him pleadingly. 'You are the only reason I'm here.' For some moments, neither of them said a word. Debra racked her brain for something meaningful to say – she'd had the best of intentions, why couldn't she explain them to the man she loved? Tears threatened to rise, and she gulped them down fiercely, but it was hard to hide her disappointment. This was just like all their conversations of the past months. Or rather, lack of conversations.

The hurt didn't leave Nicholas's eyes – if anything, a

sort of earnest consternation intensified it. 'Do you not trust me? Did you think I was having –'

She pressed her fingers against his lips. 'No, Nicholas. No, I never thought that.' With a light caress, she withdrew her hand. 'When we first met, you remember? I was a waitress too, only ...' She threw a look down at her outfit.

He followed her gaze and frowned. 'I don't understand what Ol' Flannery's has got to do with ...' He let his sentence trail off, shook his head and fixed his stare at a point on the wall. 'Doesn't matter now,' he said. 'I think you should leave.' His gaze returned to her face, impenetrable and dark.

She pursed her lips and shook her head.

Nicholas's eyes flashed impatiently. 'Debra, I don't know what you're trying to achieve with this nonsense, but please call a cab and –'

'Would you come with me?' she asked, not missing a beat.

'You know I can't do that. I'm here for work.'

Debra raised her chin. 'So am I.' She turned on her heels and left him standing there. She felt his eyes follow her all the way back to the bar.

'Two Gibson Martinis,' she told the barman and went to take another order. Al was talking animatedly; she could see his watch, so swanky it flared even in the dim light, a stark contrast to Nicholas's face, which looked pale despite the lamps' gentle glow. His eyes burned into her when she returned to serve the drinks. Al put his arm around her waist, and she made a quick step to the side to escape his grip.

'Oh, come on, don't be shy!'

'Al!' warned Nicholas.

Al released a cavalier laugh and rose from his chair. 'Why don't you take a break and come out with me for a smoke?' he asked Debra and patted her butt.

'Sir –' Debra began as politely as she could, but Nicholas's sharp voice interrupted her.

'Get your hands off her!' he said, also rising from his seat.

A dour streak glared across Al's eyes. 'You don't mind, doll, do you?' He pulled her closer. She averted her face as the strong stench of tobacco in his breath assaulted her senses.

Nicholas pulled him away from her. 'I said leave her alone!'

'Stop it, you –' Al snarled, lunging towards Nicholas.

'Nicholas!' Debra screamed as the punch landed on her husband's face. She saw him tumbling backwards, but he didn't fall.

After a moment of utter silence – it seemed to Debra that even the music had stopped playing – a big man in a black suit appeared out of nowhere.

'Everything all right?' he asked, his stern look falling

squarely on Debra. He barely waited for her to nod before turning to the two men. 'I'll have to ask you to leave,' he said curtly.

Nicholas didn't deign to look at him. His eyes were on his wife, who made a show of putting down the tray she was holding in order to hide the overwhelming smile that had forced its way onto her face. When she looked up again, her face was solemn, but the glow in her belly was still there, and it only intensified when Nicholas put his arm around her and headed for the exit, not looking back once.

She studied the reddish swelling underneath his eye. 'Are you OK?' she asked.

He nodded once, his jaw clenched. Debra shivered. Silently, he took off his jacket and put it around her shoulders.

'Thank you,' she said with a tentative smile.

He nodded again, his eyes already on one of the cabs parked outside the club. Debra climbed through the door he held open for her and watched him take the seat next to her. They drove for several minutes without exchanging a word, the sound of the city's nightly buzz passing into the cab from the streets around them.

Debra pulled the jacket a bit closer around her shoulders.

'Are you cold?' Nicholas asked.

She looked up, happiness rushing through her, and

shook her head. Nicholas's face had lost its stony expression, and she thought she could even make out a trace of amusement in his eyes.

She wasn't mistaken. She watched as a grin began to tug at the corners of his mouth. 'I guess that's one guy I won't be working with!' he eventually burst out, then started to laugh.

His deep, boisterous laughter was a shock to Debra after what had happened in the past hour, but as she continued to watch her husband emit peals of loud, carefree guffaws, she couldn't help but eventually join in. The cab driver watched dumbfounded in the rearview mirror as his passengers shook with wild, convulsive laughter.

Admiration shone in Nicholas's eyes as, still chuckling, he gently pulled the wig from Debra's head. The cab stopped in front of their home. Nicholas pressed a fleeting kiss on his wife's mouth, paid the driver and helped her out of the car.

He didn't let go of her hand until they were inside, where Debra kicked off her heels, stripped off her gloves, fetched an ice pack and ran a cloth under cool water. Nicholas watched her as he undid his tie.

'Sit down,' she said, placing the damp cloth against his cheek.

He put his hands on her waist. 'Why were you there?'

'Because I'm a woman,' she said. 'I'm *your* woman.'

'Did I ever make you doubt that?'

13

She sighed. 'I wanted you to see me differently.'

He moved his hands around her waist. 'But I don't need to see you differently.' He gently pulled away the hand that was tending his bruised cheek and waited for her eyes to settle on his. 'I don't. Please forgive me for making you feel that way.'

She ran her fingers through his hair. 'I'm sorry for embarrassing you. And making you lose that deal.'

Nicholas shrugged. 'He was a jackass anyway.' He pulled her closer to him. 'And you could never embarrass me. I'm proud of what you did, actually.'

'Proud?' There was that smile again, forcing its way onto her face. But this time she didn't hide it.

He pulled her onto his lap. 'I should have fought for us, like you did tonight.'

She cupped his face and kissed him, melting into his lips so deeply that she couldn't suppress a moan of protest when he eventually made to rise from the chair. But he quickly turned her protest into sighs of contentment by kneeling down before her and beginning to massage her feet. Debra leaned back. 'That's what you used to do when I came home from work,' she said.

He smiled. 'And you were as ticklish as a –'

His words were drowned by her giggles as he tickled the bottom of her feet, ducking as Debra kicked him. 'Stop it!' she squealed and wriggled her legs, shooting a pout at her husband. 'Leave it to you to kill the moment!'

'I killed the moment?' He raised his eyebrows.

'You killed the moment.'

'Bummer. I wonder if I can get it back?'

'I doubt that,' she said, crossing her arms.

He pushed her legs apart and positioned himself on his knees between them. 'A challenge?'

The lust sparkling in his dark eyes sent little tingles down her back. She bit her bottom lip and smiled coquettishly.

'Hm,' he said, fidgeting around the small ribbon at the top of her corset. 'I think I'm a bit out of practice.'

Debra had to laugh. He shot her a boyish look, then started to pull open the laces, one by one. The hook and eye closures came undone with little pops, and each inch of naked skin revealed by the receding material was greeted with a kiss. Nicholas slid his hand underneath the tight folds of her leotard and cupped her breast. Her rigid nipple slipped between two of his fingers and he rolled it until her back arched in the chair and the scent of her arousal filled his nose.

His fingertips brushed the flimsy lace of her thong as he opened the bottom part of the leotard. His eyes fixed on her face, he ran his finger along her pussy. He held still for a moment, then moved the tip of his finger ever so slightly, stopping at the spot where her bated breath told him she felt his tease the most. She spread her legs a bit more. 'You haven't forgotten any of my weak spots.'

He straightened up so his face was close to her ear and whispered: 'And I haven't forgotten how they taste either.'

She uttered a little moan and then another as his palms rubbed her lips through the lace of her underwear. He withdrew his hand and slowly rolled the net stockings down her legs. Next, he placed a trail of little kisses up her leg, then pressed his nose into her lap. Debra heard a muffled sigh followed by a drawn-out groan. His breath pressed hot and damp against her skin. She buried her fingers in his hair and bent over to kiss him. 'I love you so much,' she whispered into his black strands.

Nicholas looked up at her, cupped her face in his hands and drew her into a long kiss. He rose from the floor, took her in his arms and carried her to their bedroom. The leotard was stripped off, then the thong, and Nicholas gazed at his wife's naked body: the lovely curved hips that swayed so smoothly when she danced, the pit of her navel that was so sensitive to his tongue's touch, and her breasts, rounder ever since she had become a mom, and graced with greyish blue stretch marks. He bent over her and traced the ripples with his fingers, listening to her sigh as he very carefully drew the outline of her nipples. He soaked up that which he hadn't taken the time to enjoy in so long. Languidly, his fingers ran over her breasts, moved down to her navel and then back up again, his eyes fixed on Debra's face.

She tugged at the belt of his slacks. 'Get naked,' she

16

whispered and, without moving much, he did. He stripped off his shirt, removed his trousers, shed his boxer briefs. He cupped her delta and, although his hand lay still on her wiry curls, Debra's breath sped up. He bent lower and kissed her breast. His lips enclosed her nipple, and he gently sucked at it. His bangs tickled her skin as his tongue licked her – deliberate, titillating. Hot darts shot towards her clit until the throbbing became so overwhelming she had to bite her fingers in order to hold back the moans building in her throat.

Nicholas stopped and looked at her. He tilted his head and with a grin pulled her hand away. The silence had become such a habit, Debra couldn't even remember the sound of her own voice when she relinquished her composure. 'You don't have to be quiet tonight,' whispered Nicholas, placing a tender kiss on the tip of each nipple.

She let out a soft moan. 'More,' he demanded. Lovingly whispering her name, he pushed two fingers into her pussy and watched her let go. She groaned loudly and cried out when he crooked his fingers inside her. He watched her writhe beneath him for a while before withdrawing his hand. His fingertips stroked her pussy lips, changing course whenever they came close to her clit, never touching it.

Debra shifted underneath him. Her fingernails dug into his shoulders and arms as she clutched at an outlet for the pulsating of her clit. 'Please ...'

17

'Please what?' he asked, breathing a kiss on her dry lips.

She threw him a reproving glance. 'You know what I want you to do.'

He nuzzled at her earlobes. 'Oh, I know, baby.' He kissed her temple. 'But I want to hear you say it.' His fingers circled the entrance to her pussy and pushed forwards only so much as was necessary to lure a frustrated groan from Debra's mouth.

'Touch my clit,' she whispered.

He changed neither the position of his fingers nor their pace.

'Touch my clit,' she repeated and raised her body with a rapt moan when he finally complied. 'Touch me, touch me …' she said, her voice fading. She stopped him before she lost control completely. 'Love me, please,' she whispered, fondling the nape of his neck.

Finally, she was lying underneath him again, feeling his weight on top of her, being owned by him in a way she would only allow him to own her. Eyes locked with hers, he entered her and began to rock her slowly. He watched her lips quivering, uttering sweet, lustful moans as their bodies fell back into the familiar rhythm.

Emotions washed over her, demanding tears as well as smiles. She pressed her lips against Nicholas's shoulder and held onto his body. She could feel her sweat mingling with his, she could feel his palm against hers as their fingers entangled and his breath dampened her neck.

She could feel the shudder that ran through his body before his muscles tensed and he thrust into her once more, breathlessly uttering her name as he finally let go, uniting with her in a culmination that shook them both.

Panting, Nicholas collapsed onto her body. He buried his face in her neck and didn't move. Debra relished the feeling of his warm come filling her and his cock slowly shrinking inside of her.

'I want to stay like this for ever,' she whispered as waves of cosy fatigue replaced the tremors of pleasure that had left her flesh so wonderfully satisfied.

'So do I,' he said, stroking her face. 'But I guess as often as we can will have to do.'

She wrapped her arms around him tighter. 'Is that a promise?'

Nicholas kissed the tip of her nose. 'It's a promise.' He rolled over and wrapped their bodies into the blankets. 'I love you,' he whispered into her hair. 'And I love what you did tonight. But can I ask you one favour? Please never do it again.'

Debra laughed and kissed his shoulder.

'Will they let you keep the corset though?'

'It's mine.'

Nicholas let out a content grunt before closing his eyes. Debra watched him fall asleep. Without touching it, she traced the bruised patch above his cheekbone. Tomorrow, watching him shave would excite her even more.

'Nicholas?' she whispered.

He mumbled drowsily.

'Do you still have that aftershave lotion I like so much?'

'Hmh.' He drew her close into an embrace. A trace of stubble tickled her bare shoulder, and she laughed softly against his skin.

Shutterbug
Mina Murray

When Howard recounts the story of how he and Amy first got together, he tells people it began with New Year's resolutions and ended in love. As with most unreliable narrators, there are a number of details he omits. But that's where I come in.

Howard Venn was not the type of man likely to be cast in the role of romantic lead. Statisticians are generally under-represented in cinema and Howard's footwear alone was enough to disqualify him. Pairing orthopaedic sandals with white socks, Howard carried himself with a punctilious bearing that said simply *pedant*. To most people, he looked like an ascetic. But then most people didn't know that Howard had spent the last hour of this rainy Monday afternoon hunched over in the supply room on Level 3 of the Baker &

Sons building, wanking over pictures of Amy that he wasn't supposed to have.

Howard had not had much luck with women. He found it too intimidating to approach them out of the blue, without a formal introduction. Howard preferred structured environments. He had signed up to several adult education classes in the past few months, such as *Still Life for Beginners, Part 1: Fruit* and *How to Get Your Game On* (although he never ended up attending that one). He also enrolled in a salsa class for singles, rationalising that everyone would know why they were *really* there, thus forestalling the awkwardness and recriminations with which his attempts at seduction were usually met.

The consensus among the class was that Howard led well and always maintained a perfect frame, but would never set the world on fire. Howard had picked up on this, of course, and could only look on with a mixture of detachment and despair as one by one the students paired off. Brent – a fortysomething-ish man with a bad comb-over who was almost as wide as he was tall and could not get through a single song without sweating through the back of his cheap polyester shirt – seemed to fare particularly well. Howard was at a loss as to the source of Brent's unusual magnetism. When he made discreet inquiries with his fellow students, they replied that Brent had *personality*, Brent was *fun*. No one had ever told Howard he was fun.

By the end of the course, Brent had succeeded with not one but two of the female students. Howard wondered how such an arrangement could possibly work. Having little experience in these matters, he could only assume it would operate as some sort of sexual time-share where each woman got precisely half of one week, and alternate weekends. Howard did not imagine this would be a particularly satisfying state of affairs for any woman. But then he could not imagine one woman, let alone two, being attracted to Brent, so clearly there was more than one part of the equation he hadn't solved.

The upshot of all this was that Howard was the only man left standing alone at the end-of-class dance, in a red sequined shirt that caught the light like a disco ball, and a pair of trousers so tight he feared he'd caused himself permanent testicular damage.

Across town, Amy Jenssen was having a similarly disheartening evening. She had been harangued into a striptease class by her well-meaning friend Celine, who thought that it would improve Amy's self-esteem. She had ignored Amy's protestations that having to gyrate in front of floor-to-ceiling mirrors – next to women more lithe and coordinated than herself – in little more than a feather boa and underpants would likely be counter-productive. But Celine was determined, and so Amy gave in.

Tonight was the final night of class, when each student

was to invite their significant other and perform for them a routine they had learned over the past month. Not having a significant other, Amy performed her lap dance to an empty chair.

Both Howard and Amy had resolved that *this* would be the year they found love, but at the six-month mark, things were not looking so good. Amy had been on one failed blind date after another and Howard had not fared much better. Neither, though, had considered an office romance. Sure, they had shared a brief kiss under the mistletoe at last year's Christmas party, but the punch had been heavily spiked, and it was a kiss executed with more enthusiasm than skill, the clunky frames of Howard's glasses colliding with Amy's own in a graceless plastic *pas de deux*.

When Howard sees Amy in the photo and framing store the evening after the salsa dance ball, he hides behind a display case. It's not that he dislikes her – quite the opposite, in fact. He still remembers their kiss with fondness (and bewilderment at his uncharacteristic bold-ness). But, after his demoralising evening, the last thing he wants to do is put himself out there. And Amy – who isn't in the mood for company either – is concentrating intently on which photos to print at the self-service kiosk. She stares at the screen in indecision, and casts furtive glances over her shoulder before finally confirming her selection. When a shop assistant stops to ask if she needs any help, she blocks his view of the screen with her body. Howard watches in fascination as a pinkish blush creeps up her milky-white neck. When she hurriedly gathers up the photos and stuffs them into her bag, he can't help but wonder what she has to hide. He won't be wondering long.

In her haste, Amy hasn't finalised her session properly. The machine has begun to print a duplicate set of photos and shows no signs of stopping. Howard knows it will charge Amy's credit card with each frame it prints, and as there are no staff nearby he steps in, cancels the operation himself and collects the extra prints. Most of Amy's photos are happy snaps, innocuous enough. But not all of them. The last three are experiments for Amy's erotic self-portraiture class (another of Celine's bright ideas).

The first of this triptych is a picture of Amy dressed as a harem girl, in a costume that to most people wouldn't be terribly risqué. But it is to Howard, accustomed as he is to seeing Amy in her regulation business shirt-and-skirt combo. He examines the image in detail, trying to determine if Amy has underwear on beneath her filmy blue trousers, and, if so, what colour.

In the second picture, Amy wears a lacy black skirt and a tight beige sweater that plunges into a deep vee between her ample breasts. She's lying atop a heavy oak desk and her shapely legs are stretched up into the air at a right angle to her body. Howard's gaze travels along the long line of her pins, past her lacy stocking-tops and over her neatly crossed ankles. When he sees her shiny black Mary Janes with their stiletto heels, his cock jumps in his trousers. It jumps even higher when he sees the way Amy's back is arched, her head hanging just a little over the edge of the desk, her brown eyes staring directly at him through her spectacles, the epitome of the naughty librarian, every bibliophile's pin-up girl. There's a sign on the desk saying 'Shhh', and Amy has a finger pressed up to her crimson-painted mouth.

The last photo is the most revealing. It shows Amy facing the camera, legs spread wide as she sits astride a wooden chair. All she's wearing is a satiny red bra, a black underbust corset and frilly red panties. Her tiny waist is whittled down to practically nothing by the bones of the corset, her already generous breasts and hips and ass now the obscenely exaggerated curves of fertility statues. Her feet are bare, which Howard finds hopelessly erotic. He wants to drop to his knees and suck on her pretty pink toes.

He finds himself now in a rather awkward position. For one thing, he has an erection. And he doesn't know what to do with the photos. He can't leave them there for some stranger to find, but he can't give them to Amy at the office either, for reasons that are obvious. So he carries the photos with him when he goes to the framing counter to pick up his Still Life achievement certificate, then heads back to his empty apartment.

The next day Howard brings the photos with him to work. To leave them at home would be an admission that he intends to keep them, and he knows that would be wrong. He puts the innocent photos into his filing cabinet, but dares not leave the others there. Those he carries on his person at all times. He promises himself he'll return the whole set to Amy today. All he has to do is wait until he knows she'll be away from her desk, and leave them in her drawer. She gets the photos back, he gets to remain anonymous. Simple. Except that the pictures are so bewitching he can't bear to part with them, even though they're burning in a hole in the pocket of his jacket and the longer he keeps them the guiltier he feels.

But guilty isn't all Howard feels. Whenever he closes his eyes, he sees Amy. He can't concentrate on his work; he sends the wrong reports to his clients; he is afraid to stand up because he is hard, again. To his growing consternation, Howard realises there is only one way to deal with this sort of problem.

Carrying a file in front of him for cover, he heads down the long hallway to the supply room at the end of his floor. Checking carefully to make sure no one sees him, he unlocks the door with his master key and flicks on the light. An anaemic glow illuminates the steel shelves lining the walls. There is a single chair in the room, used by the clerks when they do stocktaking, but other than that the room is bare. It's perfect for Howard's purposes. He shuts and locks the door behind him, then takes the photos of Amy out of his pocket and lines them up, reverentially, on one of the shelves closest to the light. His belt makes a clanking sound when his trousers hit the floor.

Howard likes to draw out his pleasure, so he strokes himself through his white Y-fronts to start off with, tracing the outline of his cock under the fabric. The cotton feels good against his skin, and he uses the material to increase the friction on his shaft. Only when he feels ready to burst does he free his cock. A clear drop of pre-come rests on the tip: Howard rubs the pad of his index finger over it. He licks his palm to make it wet, wraps it around his shaft and jerks off gently, staring all the while at Amy's photographs. Would she like watching this? he wonders. Would she like the way he's now gripping his shaft with both hands? The way he's leaning back and pumping his hips up and down, thrusting his cock up into the ever-tightening grip of his own two fists?

His gaze flits between the three photos. He can't say which one he prefers, but the one where Amy's finger rests against her red red lips captivates him right now. He snatches it off the shelf, holding it up close to his face.

'Amy,' he moans, imagining that sweet mouth on him, her long strawberry blonde hair brushing over his thighs, 'oh, Amy, yeah, suck me.'

Howard is about to come – his balls are drawn up tight to his body, his thighs clenching rhythmically. He takes his hand off his cock for a moment to pull up his singlet. He hadn't thought to bring tissues with him and he's too focused on the impending explosion of his orgasm to remember that the reason it's called a *supply* room is because it stores supplies. Like tissues.

It is at this moment that a key sounds in the lock and the door swings open to reveal the object of his fantasies, in the flesh. But Howard is too far gone to stop.

'I'm sorry,' he gasps, as he ejaculates over his rippling stomach, 'so, so sorry.'

Amy is dumbstruck. There is a lot for her to take in. First, that Howard has *those* pictures of her, which she never thought to show to anyone. Second, that everything she thought she knew about him was wrong. And third, that even if she can't see all of him because of the shadow she's casting, Howard is *hot*. Amy doesn't know how she never saw that before, never saw beyond the spreadsheets and the sandals.

Cheeks burning with shame, Howard pulls up his trousers and stumbles past her without a word. Amy knows she should feel outraged, but all she feels is aroused. Oh, and flattered. She has never considered herself beautiful, with her too-big nose and her slightly lopsided smile. When she picks up her photos and looks at them again, really looks at them, she sees how wrong she is. She may not be perfect, but that doesn't mean she's not beautiful. For the rest of the day Amy walks around as if she's high.

Howard is not in the next day, though, or the day after that, or for the rest of the week. Amy begins to worry that he's not coming back. She asks around, but no one has heard from him. So she bribes the temp in Human Resources – more boobs than brains – and gets Howard's private email address. She has to let him know that everything is OK, that even if she is puzzled about how he got the photos, she isn't angry with him. And she knows just how to prove it.

When Amy gets home that night, she takes three more self-portraits, each in a different style – one stereotypically 'sexy', one classy and the other explicit – because she doesn't know what Howard would like best. That remote shutter gadget she thought she'd never use is certainly coming in handy. After a quick shot of whisky for courage, she sends Howard an email, attaching the three original photos that he has already seen, and the new ones she's just taken.

To: Howard Venn
From: Amy Jenssen
Subject: Photos
Attachments: Amy.zip

Here's the complete set. If you like what you see, meet me at Pirelli's for dinner tomorrow night at 8pm.

We missed you this week.

Amy

Howard has spent the last four days in his apartment, too ashamed to go to work, trawling the internet for advice on appropriate wording for an apology card. He sees Amy's email immediately, and his stomach lurches. He's sure the attachment will be a copy of the complaint Amy plans on lodging with management. Not that he blames her. He is thoroughly disgusted with himself.

He has to read the message three times before its meaning sinks in. She *won't* be making a complaint. She *missed* him. She actually *wants* to see him again. With a shaky hand, Howard downloads the photos. He is of course intimately acquainted with the first three, but not with the others. Exhibit 4: Amy, straddling a chair, biting her lip seductively, dressed like a schoolgirl in a plaid skirt and white cotton shirt tied up to expose her midriff. Exhibit 5: Amy, drink in hand, blowing a kiss to the camera, in a semi-transparent chiffon peignoir that hints at the bounty beneath.

And finally there is Exhibit 6: Amy, wearing only her birthday suit, bent forward over the desk, looking back over her shoulder into the camera and winking. Howard makes a strangled sound. He can see right between her plump thighs to the blonde-furred crease

31

in between. The lips of her sex look swollen, and he knows she was aroused when she took the photo. It is only with supreme effort, and some differential calculus, that Howard manages to get his libido under control. He's saving himself for Amy.

When he arrives at the restaurant, Amy hardly recognises him. His usually tousled hair is swept back; he wears a suit and expensive Italian shoes. He searches the room for her anxiously, and when their eyes meet a broad smile transforms his usually serious face. She stands to greet him and his eyes widen at the way her red dress clings to the flare of her hips.

'Hi, Howard, I'm really glad you came.' Amy winces at her *double entendre*. 'Um, I mean, I'm so happy you're here. You look great.'

'Thanks, my brother gave me some advice on what to wear.' Howard blushes. 'I don't go out much.'

Once the waiter is out of earshot, he starts to apologise. 'Amy, I'm so sorry about everything, I –'

'It's OK, Howard.'

'No, you have to let me explain,' he insists, and the next words come out in one long rush of a sentence. 'I saw you at the print shop that night, but I was too shy to say hello, and then the assistant interrupted you and you got flustered and you forgot to stop the machine and it just kept on printing. It had already printed those photos before I stopped it, and I couldn't just leave them there. And then, last Monday when you ...' Howard finally pauses, not for breath, but because what can he possibly say that would make things all right?

'It's fine, honestly –'

'It's *so not*, what I did was wrong, it was –'

'Howard,' Amy interrupts, 'I said it's fine. I'm grateful it was you who found them, not some random weirdo. So stop apologising. And ... about that other thing ... well, it's *my* right to be upset or not. And I'm not.'

She slides a hand up Howard's thigh.

'Now, let's start our date for real.'

To Howard's delight, Amy continues to make physical contact with him throughout the evening, playfully slapping his arm when he makes an unexpected joke, letting her hand linger on his when she passes him the bread basket. He insists on paying, even though Amy demurs. He is old-fashioned, he admits. But it's the least he can do, under the circumstances.

He thanks her for a lovely evening and sees her to a cab. He makes no assumptions that Amy will sleep with him. But Amy is feeling bold. She knows what she wants; it is within her reach; she wants Howard. When he opens the door for her, she whispers in his ear 'Come with me, I want to show you my studio,' then pulls him into the cab with her.

It's only a short trip to her house, where Amy removes

her glasses and pours them some wine, and Howard follows her into her study.

'This is it,' Amy says. 'Look familiar?'

Howard's throat goes dry. He definitely remembers the desk, although, when he saw it, Amy's delectable body was draped over it.

Here goes nothing, she thinks, unzipping her dress and letting it fall to the ground with a hush.

Howard also recognises the lingerie Amy is wearing. His collar suddenly seems too tight. When she strips out of her stockings, her corset, her bra and her panties, all the air seems to leave the room.

'Amy, you're –'

'Yes?'

'– so *lovely*.'

She spins, slowly, showing off her peach of an ass. When she bends forward over the desk and looks back at Howard, the expression on his face is pure unadulterated lust.

Howard approaches lovemaking as he approaches most things in his life, with the precision required to achieve the most desirable outcome. His trembling hands move over Amy's body slowly, calculating the degree of her response to each touch, assigning each a value weighted in proportion to her pleasure.

But when Amy shimmies her hips in desperation and pleads, 'Howard, lick me, please, put your tongue in me,' she undermines any goal of orderly erotic progression and forces him to act on instinct instead. Gone are the carefully measured caresses of before. He falls on her with an intensity both thrilling and frightening. The man Amy thought she knew is gone. *This* man, behind her, who traps her against the desk, who growls when she tries to turn around, is some other person entirely.

Howard's hand presses down on the small of her back, and she feels his long tongue snaking into the hot wet core of her, his nose pressing against her anus, his fingers worrying at her clit. She comes on his face before he's even taken his coat off.

When the aftershocks have died away, he helps her to her feet.

'Wow, Howard, just, wow.'

Amy starts to undress him now, a reverse striptease of coat, tie, cufflinks, shirt. He keeps his eyes open when she kisses him, as if he's scared she'll disappear. That just makes Amy hotter. When she pulls his belt free and pushes his trousers and pants down, though, she is taken aback.

'Sweet fucking Christ, Howard! That's not a cock, that's a club!'

Amy is too shocked to watch her language. She knew it was big – she had seen his member in the half-light of the storage room, before he had turned away from her – but she didn't know it was *this* big. Nothing had quite prepared her for the sight of that magnificent *thing*, emerging fierce and flushed and swollen from the dark blond thatch of his pubic hair.

Howard looks embarrassed.

'It's OK,' he says, 'we don't have to, you know, go all the way.'

'Uh, excuse me? Of course we're going all the way.' Amy strokes the prominent ridge running up the centre of his penis with her fingernail then binds the shaft with her hand. She starts pumping it up and down in short, fast strokes.

'But I don't want to hurt you.'

'You won't hurt me. Believe me, after what you just did to me, I'm more than ready to take you.'

She sits on the desk and opens her legs wide.

'So come get me.'

Howard advances, but doesn't try to enter her yet. First he examines her, pinching and pulling and probing at her sex until he's satisfied that she is indeed wet enough. Amy whimpers and squirms when his thumb circles roughly over her clit.

'Don't move,' he growls, as he spreads apart the delicate pink frills of her cunt and pinches her bud. 'I'm not done yet.'

And with that he wrings another shattering climax from her.

He enters her while she is still coming, and with each spasm her clenching sex sucks his cock higher inside her, until he is buried deep in her, right up to the root. He cries out as her nails rake his back. She feels so good to him, so right, he doesn't know how long he's going to last. He's afraid he'll shame himself by coming too quickly, so he pulls out. It will buy him the precious seconds he needs to regain his composure.

Amy looks furious, until Howard orders her on top of him. Then she smiles like a Cheshire cat and pushes him onto his back and climbs aboard, circling the head of his cock teasingly before slamming down onto him. She arches her back to let him hit her depths, then tilts her pelvis forward and tenses her inner thighs.

'Fuck, Amy,' Howard groans, 'you're so tight.'

She fucks him fast, then slow, then fast again, refusing to let him get accustomed to her rhythm. It is maddening and she knows it. But she also knows when it is time to stop teasing and start an undulating slide up and down his cock that will wrench a release from him whether he wants to come or not. In the haze of his pleasure, Howard thinks he can hear a shutter clicking, and he shouts himself hoarse as Amy rides him, ruthless, to the end.

The Shoes
Grace Moskowitz

Call it lust at first sight: I wanted to get fucked in those shoes from the moment I saw them, singing their siren's song to me through the glass of the store window. I stopped, my stride arrested by the sight of them, gleaming black and beckoning me. I dragged my friends into the store with me, making them wait while I tracked down the elusive salesgirl and asked her if I could try a pair on in my size. When I slid my foot into the first one, I looked straight down and the angle of the top of my foot, criss-crossed by the broad elastic straps, made me feel my heartbeat throb in my throat. I knew these shoes would be perfect. I knew I had to have them.

I've been a fan of stilettos since I met Victor, an old boyfriend who had infected me with his enthusiasm. It was from him that I learned of their power, not only over a man, but over myself as well. I thrilled to the contradictory feelings of vulnerability and power that wearing high heels gave me.

Victor told me and showed me that it wasn't the trampy bad-girl associations with spike heels that made the sight of a woman wearing them force thoughts of urgent and ferocious sex to course through his mind and body; for him, a woman in heels conjured up more than just thoughts of trollop/dominatrix.

It was the contradictions inherent in a woman wearing high heels that appealed to him.

He taught me that it was the contrast that affected him so strongly, the contrast of the woman's elegance and grace and the vulnerability that threatened to overtake her when her pace and agility were constrained by unstable narrow heels; her gait shaky, her feet arched dramatically to show her calves to greatest effect. He can do anything to her when she's so beautifully hampered, and she is utterly defenceless against either his need or her own stroked and fanned desires. Just as Victor saw careful construction as an irresistible invitation to deconstruction, elegance as begging for defilement, grace as needing to be disgraced, he responded to the dichotomies of femininity that were aroused when he saw a woman wearing stilettos. Both images of woman were simultaneously present, conspiring to get him hot and hard. With stilettos, a woman approaches iconic femininity and grace, underscoring the man's rough maleness. To him, when a woman wore high heels, the extremes of masculinity and femininity were emphasised. And his response to perceived feminine weakness was twofold and immediate. Something about female vulnerability aroused both his protective tendencies and his consuming need to exploit that vulnerability, to take control of her body, her will. Her responses would be beyond her control, dictated solely by him. The shoes give her elegance and in the elegance is an invitation to defile. Lipstick is there to be smudged. Mascara is there to run. Beautifully styled hair is there to be pulled and dishevelled. High heels are a constant reminder of that ambiguity.

At his insistence, the heels always stayed on.

Teetering, unsteady, riven by lust, I would lean towards him, or, thrown off-centre by too sudden or swift a step, fall against him, needing to be rescued, needing to be ravished. I'd look at my legs, lengthened by the stilettos, my shiny scarlet toenails accented with the criss-crosses of strappy sandals. The arch would shorten the perceived length of my feet, feminise and round them. I felt delectable, sultry and tempting, a victorious vixen, an enchantress and goddess of the sensual: regal, commanding, hotter than hell. In short, I felt like someone completely different.

But that was standing. It's a paradox: standing in heels makes you more vulnerable, less steady, yet you feel more powerful, more in control, the essence of feminine supremacy. When you're lying down in heels you are no longer in danger of falling, the physical problem of hampered mobility no longer exists, but the increase in psychic exposure rises in inverse proportion to the security of your 'stance'. Supine, I gave myself over to sensation. I lost my authority, or let it be taken from me, as I gave myself over to drifting down the dark current of desire. I don't know whether I surrendered myself to the Bad Girl lurking inside me or Victor turned me into one, but when I wore high heels lying down, when I glimpsed them against the mattress or the heels became tangled in the sheets, there was no doubt that I was one, that I behaved as she did, and more importantly was driven by the same always gratified desires as she was.

Victor had encouraged my purchases and enriched my collection, which included pumps with impossibly skinny silver metal spiked heels, high-heeled and high-topped boots, lacy or strappy stiletto sandals, and criss-cross, kinky-ballerina shoes with wide leather straps to wind around an ankle and calf, inspiring thoughts of both graceful dancers and raw bondage. I discovered that it was precisely this juxtaposition of class and trash that embodied the appeal of high heels. To wear them made me ultra-feminine, graceful and ethereal; it also made me earthy and sensual, vulgar and direct. I owned several pairs of what would have been demure, ladylike pumps if not for the height of their heels or the angle to which

41

they pitched my body. I became a high-heel devotee; hell, even my rain boots were a pair of shiny black vinyl spike-heeled ankle boots, whose heels were made of rubber.

But it had been a long time since I had added to my shoe rack. After Victor and I had broken up, I hadn't had someone who appreciated the allure of high heels enough to justify my breaking my budget to buy a tempting new pair. Besides, I had plenty of old favourites to wear to the theatre and to dinner, to nights out with the girls, and to enliven otherwise boring meetings. I had a good variety to wear not just to incite admiration and lust from friends, co-workers, acquaintances and strangers, but also strictly for myself, for my own sensual enjoyment, walking into a café with a magazine to grab a selfish hour of latte-fuelled dalliance, feeling inspired and inspiring as I luxuriated in decadent deviance. And in addition to the defiance of reading the latest *New Yorker* when I should have been working, wearing a pair of sexy shoes and drinking a rich and slightly bitter drink, I also wore them when I was back home, alone on my bed, wearing nothing else, rubbing my aching clit to a lather, pressing the heel of my hand up into my pulsing pussy. I guess you could say that Victor's shoe appreciation had rubbed off on me.

When I saw the pair in the window, I knew I had to have them. It had been far too long since I'd been this excited about footwear. I was pleased and surprised to learn that the shoes were priced reasonably. I guess the manufacturer figured shoes like this weren't going to get much actual wear and tear, and thus didn't need to be made with pricey materials. But that just enhanced their appeal. There's such a thing as being a Bad Girl, and then there's plain old fiscal irresponsibility; it's nice when one of these conditions doesn't necessitate the other. *Fetish on a Fixed Income*: if I'd written the book, those shoes could be the centrefold. And the fact that the shoes were cheap – literally – underscored the part of their appeal that was predicated on the fact that they were the footwear of a cheap woman – a tramp, even. These were not the classy footwear of my sueded-silk slingbacks with the gathered and pointed toes; they didn't confer elegance or sophistication, delicacy or fine-boned, highly strung beauty. These shoes proclaimed their origins; they announced the wearer's designs and motives. These shoes screamed of sex.

They flaunted their low class. They revelled in their purpose: to get you hard or wet, to turn your thoughts immediately and irrepressibly to hard, grunting, animalistic fucking.

So I bought them. And I wore them – to dinners, to parties, alone in my bed. Then I waited for the right man to wear them for.

And waited.

One guy I met was so self-conscious about his height that I couldn't even wear low heels when we went out.

While under some circumstances I would have enjoyed feeling like an Amazon, towering extravagantly over my lover, he, I could tell, would feel all his masculinity drain away at the sight of my stature, and I would end up envisioning him as a bug I could crush under my sexy foot.

I thought for a little while that Arthur, a guy I dated briefly, might be in sync. But the first time I undressed yet left the shoes on, he seemed disconcerted.

'Um ... your shoes are still on,' he noted.

'I know,' I purred. 'Isn't it hot?'

'Yeah, I guess so,' he said, dubiously.

And then he looked anxiously at the sheets as if I'd soil or tear them. We didn't go out long.

Then I met Mark, a furniture restorer who was performing a miracle on a friend's family heirloom when I first saw him, the tattoo of the 1940s pin-up, naked except for her retro pumps, smiling at me suggestively from the swell of his left bicep.

'Why that tat?' I asked, meaning, 'What 1940s cheesecake actress do you drool over?'

'Because The Shoes Stay On,' he answered, staring into my eyes with a challenge. I felt my face get hot as I murmured something in reply. We had a chance to try out his creed. Me naked and exposed, legs spread wide, pussy open and ready; him making his way from my strong thighs, past ankles circled in leather, to the arch, lifted by the shoe, and the heel, resting on the stiletto point sheathed in leather. I admired the way my legs looked, elongated, resting on his shoulders as he plunged into me; I got hot looking at my feet, toes kept pointed, feet arched, level with his ears.

But although Mark knew his way around my body as if he had written the owner's manual, it soon became obvious that owners' manuals were the only reading material he was familiar with. He thought books were for propping up stereo speakers, couldn't tell Dante from Dentyne, and I soon said goodbye to him and his shoe admiration.

When I had a date with Jackson, I didn't try to bring up the topic. But after several dates I got the feeling that my shoes would be appreciated, that keeping the shoes on would go over more than all right. We had a date set for Friday night; I began on Thursday to prepare myself.

Long ago, I differentiated between women who get fucked and women who allow themselves to get fucked. Initially, I thought I belonged to the latter. But as I reflected further, I realised that there was a third choice: that there are women who get fucked, women who allow themselves to get fucked, and women who arrange to be fucked. There is no violation for someone who is willingly violated. As I was in that last category, all my preparations were directed towards that end. Everything had, as its goal, my getting fucked. This had always been the case; I'd always assumed that the ultimate goal was to inspire lust, to make a man interested, to keep him in my thrall; but, if I were being honest, I'd have to refine that thought. I put the prep time in, not merely to attract a man and drive him mad with longing, but because, if I did it well, I'd be supremely well fucked. And I wanted that to happen.

'Tell me how you prepared your pussy for me,' Victor used to rasp. I'd tell him, and the preparations would start far earlier and be far more extensive than he'd have realised.

'I wear makeup to make my eyes look dark and inviting,' I'd say. 'I make sure that my underwear is lacy or silky, that it teases and torments my nipples and my clit, keeping them aroused and waiting for your touch. I get Brazilian waxes, baring myself entirely to the scrutiny of a woman whose eyes I can barely meet, enduring embarrassment and discomfort so that, when I am with you, you can see everything, so that there is no barrier, not even that provided by hair, to our bodies' coming together.' I'd tell him that even as I lay on a tissue-paper-covered table, my fingers holding my lips open, I'd imagine it was his cock rather than hot wax that I'd feel at that invitation. I'd tell him about the rest of the hair removal, shaving my legs so they'd be soft and silky to his touch, about choosing clothes for the amount of flesh they'd reveal and conceal, about keeping an eye on how easily they could be removed. I'd tell him about choosing shoes to arouse him, and knowing that while some girls got fucked *because* of the shoes they wore, some girls wore those kinds of shoes *hoping* that it would lead to a good fucking. It was knowing what those preparations were for that initially eroticised them, for me as well as for Victor. Now, the act of stroking on eyeshadow, or shaving my legs, frequently sent a shiver of desire through me. Preparing myself to be the object of erotic attention became a form of foreplay, taking place in solitary, hours before I could expect to be satisfied.

I was definitely in the market for a good fucking now, I thought as I sat in the nail salon, having cherry-red polish lacquered on to my toenails, the glossy hard shine turning them into a row of delectable candy apples. With the bright red shine of my toenails set off against the glossy black patent leather of my newest, steepest, sexiest shoes, I would feel like a vixen – or a goddess. With every grooming ritual I performed to make me irresistible to Jackson, my desire grew. By the time the date began, I was poised at the top rung of that extended slide into orgasm.

My preparations in place, I was a quietly seething figure of lust by the time Jackson was due to pick me up for our Friday-night dinner. His eyes lit up appreciatively when I came to the door, and his glance took me in from tousled hair to painted toes, my crimsoned nails peeping through a window made by the criss-crossed straps. I'd worn high heels when we'd gone out before, but never these, which couldn't cloak their nature under the cover of mere fashion. And always, before, no matter how sexy my shoes, I'd taken them off before we had sex. But I could tell, by the way his eyes lingered on my footwear, that there would be no objection to the shoes staying on tonight. I could see myself as vixen/goddess reflected in his gaze, and knew that I would be worshipfully defiled. We wouldn't be having that cup of coffee after dinner.

All through the dinner at the quiet, intimate restaurant, I sat angled in my chair so that my crossed legs were adjacent to the table rather than under it. Seeing my own legs and feet thus displayed, coupled with the flirtatious banter and simmering looks passing between us, pushed me to a state of arousal that was becoming obvious. My nipples poked stiffly through my lacy bra and were clearly visible, gumdrops tenting the thin fabric of my blouse. I shifted in my chair, hiking my skirt higher up my thighs. My panties were so damp that I knew when we left there would be a wet spot on my seat. Leaving, I turned around and checked: there it was, broadcasting my desire to the busboy, waiter, and whoever the seat's next occupant was. I flushed; was it shame or the exhibitionism-fuelled level of arousal that made my cheeks pinken?

The car ride back to my house was a blur. As I slid the key into the lock, I felt him behind me, sliding his hands up my body to lay the flat of his palms on my breasts, pushing his groin against the small of my back. His head bent against mine as he pressed his nose into my neck and inhaled deeply, smelling my skin and perfume, making that skin a little hotter.

Once over the threshold, I turned around in his embrace, our mouths coming together searchingly, hungrily. Encircling him with my arms, I pressed him into me, feeling the muscles in his ass clench slightly in response to my touch as he pushed against me. Jackson put his hand up under my blouse and cupped my breast in its lace confines. He started to stretch the neck opening so as to get to me with his mouth, but I disengaged long enough to pull the garment over my head and drop it on the floor. I happen to like that shirt.

'What have we here?' he teased, letting his fingers brush lightly against my straining nipples. In response, I pressed myself more firmly into his grasp as I thrust my tongue back into his warm, wet mouth, and my own hands pushed up and under his shirt, feeling the play of muscles in his back. 'I'm going to fuck you so hard,' he murmured, bending his mouth to my breasts as he unclasped the bra and it fell away from me. My breasts sprang out, the nipples jutting into the cool air. I could see his cock's outline clearly against the fabric of his trousers.

'Do you want this? Hmm? Do you want me to suck your tits?' His pointed tongue flickered back and forth over those points, sending electric currents directly to my clit.

'Yes,' I sighed. You know how sometimes you just *know* it's going to be an exceptionally strong climax? I could feel the distance of the impending orgasm's slide lengthen, its rise increase to a steeper angle. 'I want it. Please.' I pressed more urgently against him, feeling his cock hard in his trousers.

He suckled one nipple hard while he lightly teased the other with his fingers and then used the flat of his hand to brush lightly but rapidly over it. As the pace of his palm's strumming grew faster, he increased the suction of his mouth, biting gently down. The simultaneous sensations of feathery teasing and forceful sucking sent a contraction through me. My legs began to grow unsteady, my head fell back and my cunt clenched and gushed as I felt my clit getting harder and more needy. I planted my legs firmly apart to keep my balance. But once Jackson moved his free hand up under my skirt, I knew I couldn't stay vertical much longer.

'Come in the bedroom,' I said, my voice betraying my desire, 'I need to lie down.'

Jackson kicked off his shoes; mine stayed on, as he took off his socks and shirt, dropping both on the floor. When he unzipped his trousers, his cock came bouncing out – he wore no underwear. I dropped to my knees and cupped his pendulous balls in my hand as I brought my face close to nuzzle his musky scent. The heady fragrance made my mouth water, and I treated his swollen tool to a few quick licks. But before I could take his cock all the way in and suck him as I wanted to, he pulled me roughly up and off him and shoved me onto the bed. First my skirt was pushed up, then yanked all the way off, as his fingers found their way around the edge of my panties and up into my wet, wet pussy. He fingered me, then brought my juices back to my clit, circling over and around, over and around. As I began to thrust my hips towards the ceiling, he withdrew, leaving me wanting. Impatiently, I tugged my panties off, while he chuckled softly. 'Can't wait, can you?' he teased. Jackson appreciates the ferocity of my hunger, especially when he frustrates it. Now I was naked except for my shoes. Jackson wore nothing at all, save for the luminescent drop of pre-come shimmering on his cockhead. I licked my lips automatically, but he kept out of reach.

'Oh, God,' he marvelled, the lust shining in his eyes. 'You are so fucking delectable. I'm going to make you come till you cry.'

'Please,' I beseeched, my voice's pitch beginning to heighten. My plea was inarticulate, unfinished; my thoughts fragmented. I wasn't capable of more language. I just knew I needed his touch, anywhere. He rewarded my entreaty with a brief dip down, a few leisurely licks, before coming back up to kiss my tang back to me. I braced myself, waiting to be roughly thrust into, or entered inch by teasing inch.

And then Jackson unbuckled and removed my right shoe.

I felt a twinge of disappointment, but in my aroused state I quickly put it behind me. This was clearly going to be a fabulous fuck, and, whether they remained on or not, the high heels had obviously done their job. Besides, I couldn't expect my every kink to be complemented by his.

But instead of dropping the shoe beside the bed and removing the other one, Jackson continued to hold it, his hand gripping it over the instep. Softly, gently, he laid the back of it, the part that encases the heel, against my cheek. The patent leather felt smooth and cool against my flushed face. 'I love your shoes, baby,' he murmured, his lips grazing my cheek a beat behind the stiletto's touch. Then he put the tip of the heel very delicately against my ear and stroked the lobe as softly as a sigh, before replacing the heel-tip with his mouth and breathing – not licking, just *breathing* – on my ear, causing my clit to jump. I began to sense the shoe as an extension of Jackson himself.

Now the heel began to journey down my neck, lightly tripping along that sensitive space. I opened my mouth, unable to speak. Softly, Jackson touched the heel to my open lips, a wordless order for my tongue to taste the gritty sole and leave my saliva on the edge of the shiny patent leather. Bringing the shoe downwards, he circled my nipple and then dragged the sharp heel down the length of my body with enough pressure to leave a visible line on my sensitive skin before his feathery tongue followed the trail, flickering like a candle's flame.

He touched the sole to the wet split of my body, spreading my juices around my open cunt. Then he brought the arch of the shoe to my clit and, looking me straight in the eye, lowered the heel until it gently caught on my inner lips. I gasped and jerked my hips upwards, my breath catching as he teased the sharp heel around the outside of my opening. I felt it scratch, but the sensation was more like scratching an elusive itch than an irritant. I didn't know whether I was terrified or more aroused than I'd ever been. Did I trust him enough? Would he hurt me?

Out, around, increased pressure on my thigh, and then the dragging of the tip towards me. I didn't dare to breathe, fearing that a quick move could result in agony. Even so, I thrilled with anticipation of an act I had never envisioned and yet now desperately wanted to experience. He held the glistening heel poised for a moment, and I realised I was straining upwards to encourage it.

Our eyes met and a soundless question was asked and answered. Holding the shoe sole upwards, Jackson slowly, excruciatingly slowly, inserted the tip of the high heel an inch or so inside me. A last twinge of fear ran through me, and was drowned by a rush of urgent desire almost painful in itself. Ever so slowly he pulled the tip back out. Then he entered a bit more deeply, a hair more forcefully. Then rocked back out. In. Out. A strand of viscous juice appeared, like the most delicate of gossamer threads, tethering the shoe to my hot and hungry hole. I lifted my hips in desperation, in invitation, and he thrust the six-inch heel all the way in, until it came to rest inside me with the sole, where the ball of my foot was supposed to rest, pressed up against my needy clit. He rocked the sole and he fucked me with the heel, his face transformed into something feral. I could feel myself climbing that last rung, reaching, reaching. I bucked harder against the shoe, hearing the slap of my wet pussy flesh against the slick, smooth leather.

'*Fuuuck,*' groaned Jackson, his face contorted with wonder and lust, and I realised that he'd been slowly stroking himself. 'Oh, fuck,' he repeated, as his finger wedged itself in between the shoe's sole and my hard clit. I exploded, my cunt closing like a clenched fist around the shoe's heel. I came into lightness so strong it was blinding. Sensing the convulsions racking me, Jackson took the heel out and rammed his steel-hard cock into me in one swift, brutal movement. I continued to come, balanced on the fine tip of existence. I wasn't aware I'd been screaming until I felt my throat, sore and strained.

Jackson groaned, pushing into my pussy more deeply still, once again following with himself the trail the shoe had started, and then bellowed as his own come gripped him.

I felt my heart beating throughout my body, the realisation seeping through me like the blood pulsing as my breathing slowed. I had misread the promise those sexy shoes had sung to me: all along I had thought that I wanted to be fucked in high-heeled shoes, when what I had really wanted was to be fucked *by* them. My head spun as I considered the implications – and all the gorgeous shoes waiting to be bought, waiting to be used.

They're called 'fuck me' shoes, after all ...

Creature Feature
Rose de Fer

The bikini-clad girl screamed as the Creature advanced, his arms outstretched and reaching for her. His reptilian skin gleamed in the moonlight, the water running over his lean, scaly chest and muscular thighs.

The girl backed away slowly, too slowly, and her pursuer caught her easily. She fainted as he lifted her in his arms and carried her off towards the lake.

After a few moments the stillness was broken by the crack of the sheriff's rifle shot.

'No!' Dan cried. 'You'll hit Barbara!'

The Creature did not turn but continued his relentless progress towards the black water of the lake with Barbara lying helpless and insensible in his arms.

'I'll try to shoot it in the leg,' said the sheriff, taking careful aim.

His shot was true and the Creature gave a howl of rage

and pain as he crumpled to his knees. Barbara tumbled free of his grasp and came to with a scream. She ran to her boyfriend as the Creature began dragging himself towards the water's edge. Gunshots exploded around him but he had reached the shelter of the overhanging rocks. He glanced back once at Barbara and there was something wistful and tender in his look. Then he dived gracefully into the water and vanished into the depths.

Barbara burst into tears, clinging to Dan. After a while she spoke, her voice a tremulous whisper. 'Do you think he'll ... come back?'

'Of course not,' Dan said, wrapping her in his arms. But there was something uncertain in his voice as he stared over her shoulder at the sheriff. 'Well? Did you kill it, Sheriff?'

The burly man moved to the edge of the lake and kicked a pebble into the water, where it made a tiny splash. 'Don't know, son,' he said gruffly. 'But they say that lake is bottomless. Alive or dead, we'll never find it.'

Barbara shifted her haunted gaze from the sheriff to the fading ripples on the surface of the lake. They seemed to go on for ever.

A dramatic music cue followed and then the words THE END appeared over the monochrome image, followed a beat later by a wavering question mark. The cast list came next and Betty smiled at the dual credit of 'Steve Winter as Dr George Bentley and THE CREATURE'.

The darkened picture house was filled with the noise of chattering and laughing as the patrons – most of them couples – got up to leave. But Betty always stayed until the lights came up. The spell wouldn't be broken until the darkness was.

She'd seen *It Came From Black Lake* six times and already she wanted to see it again.

The first time had been on a double blind date with Judy and two brothers that a friend of Judy's had set them up with. They went to the drive-in in the boys' Mustang convertible and Betty had 'ruined' the evening by not wanting to do what most teenagers did at the drive-in. Judy hadn't spoken to her since. But she couldn't help it; she only had eyes for Steve Winter. As soon as he'd appeared on the screen, a spell was cast and the boy beside her might as well have been the Invisible Man.

After that Betty went to the Palms Theatre to see it again, this time by herself. She'd watched, entranced, as the handsome Dr Bentley paddled his canoe along the shores of Black Lake. Alligators watched him pass but they left him alone as he peeled off his sweat-soaked shirt and waded into the murky water to find samples. He scooped up the gooey atomic sludge from the surface of the water and took it back to his lab, where the fateful explosion soon took place, transforming him into the Creature.

Betty had thought he was good-looking as the scientist

but as the Creature he was positively dreamy. The costume wasn't the chunky rubber monster suit worn by so many other actors in similar films. Steve Winter's costume clung to his well-defined muscles like glossy paint, enhancing his lean physique.

His face wasn't hidden behind a goggle-eyed mask either. No, the makeup artist had kept the effect minimal there, with only fins and scales to show he had become a monster. An oddly appealing one.

Betty had stayed and sat straight through the second showing, then the third. When she'd finally left that day the manager had teased her good-naturedly about her fascination. He knew a teenager in love when he saw one, he'd said, tipping her a wink.

Betty had lowered her head, blushing furiously as she hurried out into the humid Florida evening. She'd breathed in the moist air, closing her eyes as she imagined how it would feel to be captured by the Creature, carried in his strong arms to his lair. What would he do to her if she struggled? What if she tried to escape and he caught her? Would he tie her up, lash her to the jagged rocks with coils of rope? Would he whip her to teach her not to resist?

Then a passing car had beeped its horn, startling her out of her reverie before the fantasy could pick up steam. Embarrassed, Betty had hurried home. There she could continue her lustful train of thought in her own room, tucked up in bed where no one could see her. Well, no one but Steve Winter, who gazed at her from the pictures she'd clipped from *Castle of Frankenstein* magazine and tacked up on her wall.

Steve in a colour still, arms crossed, smile radiant, marine-blue eyes sparkling. Steve as Dr Bentley, frowning over the atomic particles he was looking at through his microscope. Steve as the Creature, shortly after the explosion, confronting his new self in the mirror. And, best of all, Steve as the Creature, carrying the girl in his arms towards the lake.

Of course the film – and the Creature – bore a close resemblance to another film with a similar title from a few years earlier. Betty had seen it once on television and enjoyed it, but that creature's blank fishy stare hadn't affected her the way Steve Winter's had. The Black Lake story was completely different and Betty loved the fact that it had been filmed in the Everglades, practically her own backyard. Oh, if only she'd known then! She could have gone down and watched the shooting, maybe even met Steve and got his autograph. Maybe even …

But her chance was coming. The revival showing at the Palms was partly to drum up interest in the sequel, *The Return of the Creature From Black Lake*, which the theatre manager had told her would soon be filming down in the Glades. Of course the sheriff's bullets hadn't killed him! He'd simply returned to his underwater lair to heal. Soon he would be back, driven by both passion and vengeance. Perhaps this time in search of a mate.

Betty blew Steve a kiss from her bed before turning out the light. Then her hand strayed down beneath the covers and up underneath her nightie. In her mind she was a feisty lady reporter hot on the trail of the missing scientist and determined to solve the mystery. Her search led her deep into the swamp, where one careless misstep sent her tumbling into the water of the infamous Black Lake. Where the Creature was watching, waiting. He rose up before her, water streaming over his sleek torso as he gathered her in his arms and dived with her through the inky depths. Betty held her breath until they reached the entrance to the cave and emerged into the air once more. The Creature carried her to the nest he'd made for her, sat her down and watched her intently.

She didn't resist as he stripped her naked, slitting open her wet blouse and skirt with sharp claws. She trembled as he loomed over her, examining his property, exploring every inch of her soft human skin with his webbed fingers. He gently coaxed her legs apart and stroked her sex with that intoxicating mix of curiosity, tenderness and desire, his eyes keenly observing her responses. For although the disaster in his laboratory had transformed him physically, he was still a scientist beneath the scaly skin. And now she could be his experiment.

She peered into his eyes, seduced by their piercing gaze.

Tentatively she reached up to stroke his sinewy chest. The cave glowed with phosphorous and she trailed her fingers over the sleek, gleaming muscles of his abdomen and down to his thighs, down to where his hard cock waited to fill her.

As always, Betty came before the fantasy got too intimate. What turned her on most of all was being his captive, his subject, his plaything. She loved the thought of being teased and inspected, restrained and admonished for any escape attempts. Sometimes in her mind he pinned her down on the damp cave floor, pressing his hardness against her while she struggled feebly beneath him. And sometimes he took her back to his laboratory, where he strapped her to a table and performed unspeakable experiments on her helpless naked body.

She shuddered with embarrassed pleasure as she curled into a ball, her sex throbbing from its climax. She was still a virgin and she didn't really know what actual sex would be like or how a man's cock would feel inside her. But she wanted to know, very badly. And she wanted Steve Winter to be the man to show her.

As she drifted off to sleep she was sure she could hear the voice of the Creature, calling to her from out in the Glades.

'You can stand over there, doll. Just keep your mouth shut and don't get in the way.'

The portly man wasn't the director. He was presumably someone in charge of keeping visitors to the set under control. But there was only Betty. She had been expecting an army of screaming teenage girls corralled behind a barrier, fans younger or more appealing than she was who would draw Steve's eye immediately. It was a shock to see how small the location set actually was.

There were only a few people around. The one with the megaphone who was shouting at the crew must be the director. Two men were setting up heavy camera equipment while a woman ferried cups of coffee back and forth from a van. Two trailers were parked nearby, just off the road, and Betty felt her heart give a little tumble as she realised that Steve must be inside one of them.

'Where are all the actors?' she asked, forcing herself to sound casual.

'It's just the Creature this morning,' the man replied. 'Swimming around, diving in, climbing out. Home sweet home, eh?' He nodded towards the swamp they had chosen for Black Lake. Swollen cypress trees rose from the water, hung with long tresses of Spanish moss. 'Don't know how he does it. You wouldn't get me in that water for anything, not with all them gators out there!'

'They're probably more afraid of you than you are of them,' Betty said, although she did admire Steve's fearlessness. She didn't know anyone who'd be willing to put on a wetsuit and go splashing around in the Glades, least of all herself.

'Well, I'm not taking any chances,' the man said, patting his back pocket where presumably he had a gun. 'You give a yell if you spot any, OK?'

She smiled and assured him she would, although she had no intention of watching for alligators once Steve Winter was on set. And she didn't have to wait long. Soon the door of one of the trailers opened and there he was: the Creature.

Betty's breath caught in her throat. He moved with a sinuous grace and he was even taller in person than he appeared onscreen, towering over everyone he passed on his way to the swamp. When he reached Betty he stopped for a moment and looked her up and down, just as the Creature might size up a female victim. Warmth flooded Betty's face and all her well-rehearsed greetings died on her tongue as she found herself staring mutely at him.

He looked like a statue of a Greek god dipped in blue-black ink, every taut muscle sculpted and defined by the glossy costume that clung to him like a second skin. Hours seemed to pass as Betty drank in the sight of him, her eyes roaming over every inch of his beautiful body. At last her gaze travelled back up to his face and she opened her mouth only to find she couldn't speak even a single word.

Steve's eyes gleamed with obvious amusement and she

blushed and lowered her gaze. Then he reached out one webbed hand to touch her hair. Betty gasped, both from shock and excitement, and she heard Steve chuckle softly behind the makeup. Her heart pounded and her hand fluttered at her breast. Steve's eyes were immediately drawn there and she felt her nipples stiffen beneath her the lightweight material of her summer dress. Her sex pulsed in response and when Steve began to smile she wondered if he had the same keen senses as the infamous Creature. Could he smell her arousal?

Then he moved past her and she watched him as though in a trance. She staggered back against a tree for balance as the spell slowly wore off and she began to curse herself for her starstruck idiocy. Oh, but he had touched her! Her scalp tingled from the contact and the sensation sent hot pulses of desire through her body. All her naughty fantasies flashed through her mind and she shook her head to clear it.

But as soon as she looked over at the swamp and saw the Creature striding into the water she knew it was hopeless. She could feel the wetness in her panties, the almost painful stiffness of her nipples as they strained against the confines of her dress. Every inch of her was hungry for Steve, for his piercing eyes and powerful hands.

The director shouted 'Action!' and Steve dived down beneath the surface of the water. He was lost for a few seconds and then he re-emerged slowly, rising up from the black mirror of the lake. Betty shuddered with excitement as she watched him swim to the shore and pull himself out onto the rocks. His slick costume shone in the light and Betty imagined stroking the outline of each silky muscle.

'Cut!'

The moment was broken by the director's annoyed shout and then there was some discussion with one of the cameramen. The male voices grew louder and angrier and in no time an argument had broken out. There was apparently something wrong with some piece of equipment. Betty didn't care what the problem was; she was watching Steve. He leaned against the rocks, his arms crossed in a very un-Creature-like posture, looking bored. And then he looked at her.

Their eyes met and, even though he was some distance away, she was sure she saw him smile.

'Hey, listen, guys,' he said, his deep resonant voice immediately silencing the others, 'I'm gonna take five while you fix the equipment, OK? Give me a shout when you're ready for me.'

And without even waiting for a response he headed back towards his trailer, back towards Betty.

Her legs suddenly didn't feel strong enough to hold her up. Her heart pounded in her ears as the Creature made his purposeful way across the grass and then stopped in front of her. He paused for only a moment before sweeping her up in his arms and carrying her off to his trailer. He opened the door easily and kicked it shut again behind him.

Inside was a small living space with a shadowy corridor leading off to the left. Betty wrapped her arms around Steve's neck as he carried her into the adjoining room and she began to tremble when she saw the bed. She looked up into Steve's face, hardly daring to hope this was all really happening. But the smile she saw there confirmed that she wasn't dreaming. The Creature deposited her gently on the bed and stood looking down at her.

'Well now,' he said, 'what shall I do with you?'

Betty's face burned, the deep flush spreading across her throat and chest and down through her body. Down to where she was tingling and growing very wet.

Fuck me, her mind said, giving at least a silent voice to the lewd thought she'd been having ever since she'd first set eyes on Steve Winter. Then, emboldened by his piercing gaze, she said it.

'Fuck me.'

If he seemed startled by her frankness he didn't show it. He hadn't needed her to say it anyway; her panting arousal must have been obvious from the moment they'd met.

He undressed her, unhindered by his webbed fingers. As he deftly untied the straps of her dress and slid it down to expose her breasts, Betty closed her eyes and lay back. She kicked off her shoes and raised her bottom so he could slip her white cotton panties off. She could hardly believe it was happening.

Then he lowered his head to hers and kissed her. He smelled of aftershave and latex, a kinky combination that only excited her more. His lips kissed a trail down her throat, making her shudder. She arched her back, presenting herself to him.

He took her wrists and manoeuvred them over her head. She gripped the wooden slats of the bed, writhing on the coverlet. Steve opened a drawer in the nightstand and Betty whimpered as he removed a length of rope. She pressed her legs together as a jolt of excitement shot through her and she held perfectly still as he wound the rope around her wrists and tied her to the bed. He took a step back and looked down at her, restrained and begging for him with every shallow breath.

'My, my,' he said in a silky voice, 'you are quite helpless now, aren't you?'

Another wave of lust washed over her and Betty chewed her lip, straining against the ropes and lifting her hips like an offering. Her eyes roamed over his exquisite form, travelling down to the bulge at his crotch. It swelled against the rubber and she wondered where the fastenings in his costume were. But he seemed in no hurry to undress himself.

He knelt over her and placed his hands on either side of

her face. She nuzzled against them like a pet. His gentleness belied the strength and power she knew he possessed, as though he really were the Creature, holding himself back from ravishing her. With excruciating deliberation he trailed his fingers down over her face and throat, then down the sides of her rib cage, teasingly avoiding the swell of her breasts.

Betty moaned softly as he stroked her flat belly, then teased her again by circling her sex without touching it. His hands traced her lines and curves, raising gooseflesh as he stimulated every inch of exposed skin. Every inch but the ones that craved his touch the most.

She was on the verge of demanding when at last he returned to her upper body. Her nipples stiffened painfully as he caressed her breasts and then she gasped as his fingers closed around them, squeezing. The latex felt cool and slightly clinical and she blushed furiously as she imagined herself as Dr George Bentley's experimental subject. Restrained on a cold metal table, writhing with delirious pleasure as he probed and stroked and stimulated her, observing her responses.

He tweaked her nipples, pinching them tightly until she gave a little cry. It hurt but the pain only intensified her arousal. Her sex throbbed and she squeezed her legs together, wishing he would force them apart roughly and plunge himself inside her.

But he hadn't finished playing with her.

He dipped his head and kissed her again, pressing his chest against hers. The chill of the rubber against her breasts made her nipples burn, a sensation somewhere between pleasure and pain and wholly erotic. His tongue teased hers, circling inside her mouth. Betty writhed beneath him, angling her pelvis up to the tantalising hardness he was keeping from her.

Finally she wrapped her legs around him, hooking her ankles together behind his back and urging his cock down, forcing it against her sex.

Steve broke the kiss and drew back a little, smiling down at her. Then he lowered his head to her breasts, kissing her nipples in turn. She cried out as his tongue flicked playfully over each hard little bud, sending bursts of desire through her entire body. Her sex throbbed painfully, desperate for his touch.

She heard the creak of the ropes against the wood as she strained in her bonds. His captive, his prisoner. He could do anything to her and he knew it.

At last he pulled away and her wet nipples burned at their exposure to the air. He smacked her thigh lightly and she obeyed the silent command, opening her legs for him. Steve took hold of her ankles and prised her legs wide apart, as wide as they could go.

Betty had never felt so exposed in her life. An intoxicating blend of lust and embarrassment surged through her as he pushed her legs back against her chest, making a shameless display of her wet cunt. The bulge in his costume grew as he stared frankly at her sex and Betty could see the smears of moisture from where she had pressed herself against him.

Steve lowered her feet to the bed, keeping her legs wide apart and her knees bent. Then he slipped one hand underneath her bottom and lifted her up. Betty gasped. Her legs dangled for a moment as he held her up and shoved a pillow beneath her, presenting her sex to him.

She closed her eyes as he trailed his fingers along her inner thighs, making her shiver. Then, at last, he touched her. She bit her lip as she felt the cool latex against her sex. His webbed fingers moved along her slippery folds, exploring every inch of her. When he reached her clit she cried out. After so much teasing the stimulation was almost too much. Her legs closed slightly and he forced them apart, shooting her a stern look that made her pulse quicken. Betty trembled as she waited for his touch again.

With the fingers of his left hand he spread her lips apart while he stroked her warm wet opening with his right hand. She felt a single finger slide up along the sides and around the warm centre before slipping inside. The clinical feel of the latex made her blush furiously and she clenched around him, urging him on. His left thumb moved lazily back and forth across the knot of her clit and she whimpered as her body twitched in response. But she kept her legs apart for him.

He inserted another finger, then another, all the while thumbing her clit with his left hand. Each touch sent sparks of almost unbearable pleasure through her and she cried out with each delicious surge of bliss. She could feel herself climbing, edging upwards towards a powerful climax, and she rocked her hips against Steve's hand, angling herself against him so hard it hurt. He responded, increasing the friction against her clit, rubbing it hard now, moving his fingers inside her roughly.

Betty gasped and panted beneath his ministrations, her arms quivering as she strained against the ropes, her legs trembling with the effort of keeping them spread, her body ready to scream with the overload of sensation.

And just when she thought she couldn't take any more, the pleasure peaked and she threw back her head with an animal cry as the climax overtook her. Her sex spasmed around Steve's fingers while her clit throbbed and pulsed and sent wild jolts of ecstasy through her body.

Afterwards she lay limp and exhausted in her bonds. She was so disconnected from her surroundings that when she looked up and saw the Creature she gave a little cry of surprise.

Steve laughed as he untied her and rubbed her wrists gently. 'Sorry,' he said. 'Not who you expected?'

Betty blushed. 'I guess that costume's not easy to get in and out of.'

'Oh, don't worry. The Creature could have fucked

you. I just thought he might have a little more fun with you this way first.'

'First?'

'Mm-hmm.' He smiled, his eyes shining with wicked intent. 'But Dr Bentley would like to have you as well. I think a girl's first time should be with someone fully human, don't you?'

Betty stared at him in amazement. He knew! He knew she was a virgin. Was it that obvious? It took her a while to find her voice.

'Good idea,' she said. Then she reached up to touch his face and run her hand down his rubber-clad chest. When she reached his crotch she gave it a little squeeze. 'But maybe you should bring the Creature too. In case I ... resist.'

Midnight in Faerieland
Kathleen Tudor

Emma was waiting by the front door, and she jumped when the knock sounded. She hurried to the door and her smile bloomed across her face as she saw Shane waiting on the step. She reached for the light switch and then pulled the door shut behind her, leaving her purse behind. As requested, she had only her keys and her ID, and she handed both over to Shane without a word.

He took them and kissed her, his lips moving possessively over hers. 'Good evening,' she murmured silkily when he pulled back.

Shane smiled and leaned forward to nip her lower lip one last time before answering with a 'good evening' of his own. 'You look lovely,' he said. The key rasped in and out of the lock as he secured the house.

'Anything would look good next to you,' Emma teased. She was nervous, and it always made her mouthy.

Fortunately, Shane liked that about her. He tweaked her nose, maybe just a bit too hard, and then tucked her keys and ID away in a pocket and took her arm, formally but possessively, to lead her to the car.

'I hope you're not feeling too determined to be a brat tonight,' he said, his tone teasing. With his free hand he reached for her hand where it rested on his arm. She didn't jump or squeak as his nails dug in for a moment. He followed the pinch with an affectionate pat and a wink at her, then stepped ahead of her to open the car door.

'When have you ever known me to be bratty?' she asked, looking up at him as he helped her into the car. Shane gave her an ironic look and shook his head before shoving the car door shut and sealing her inside.

Emma chuckled to herself and settled comfortably into the seat, snapping her belt into place as she waited for him to walk around the car. Her stomach tingled with feelings of anticipation and nervousness; she'd been told to dress casually, but also that tonight was going to be very important. Was she going to be tested? Was she already? Her smile slipped as she rethought the teasing and sass, but Shane hadn't seemed annoyed about it, had he?

He slid behind the wheel and reached across to pat her leg affectionately before he turned the key in the ignition, and she sighed. No, not mad. But she still had no clue what was going on, and the smile she turned on him felt forced.

When he glanced over at a red light, he apparently saw the tension that kept her stiff and still in her seat. He reached up as if to cup her face affectionately, but his fingers went to her ear instead, and he pinched the cartilage. Emma felt the wave of endorphins and the chemical cocktail of submission as it flowed through her, as if magically released from that small spot. The pain was like an anchor, hooking her into the moment and into Shane as he dropped her into subspace with a touch. Her body warmed, her sex awakening with a spark, and her spine straightened as if to show herself off to full effect. She whimpered as the feeling of tension melted out of her, replaced with awareness and an altogether different kind of anticipation.

Shane dropped his hand to the gear shift as the light turned, but the effect was complete. 'Who am I?' he asked.

'My Master,' she said, her voice already husky with her desire to please.

'And who are you?'

'Your devoted Girl,' she answered.

'And your duty?'

'To serve and please you, Master.'

'Good Girl. We're almost there.'

It didn't surprise her when he pulled into Unbridled, the dungeon where they had a membership. He parked the car, and Emma waited patiently as he got out and went around to let her out, as was proper. He'd stopped to get a bag out of the trunk, but she kept her curious thoughts to herself as she took his arm and let him lead her into the dungeon.

The foyer was tastefully decorated like any waiting room or reception, and didn't reveal anything of what went on beyond the inner doors, unless you knew enough to identify the kink flag that was pinned to the wall. An innocent-looking young man sat behind the desk reading on a Kindle, but he put it away and flashed them a smile as they stepped inside. 'Welcome to Unbridled. Do you have your ID with you?'

Shane handed over the cards with a polite nod, and the young man scanned each of them and typed for a moment before handing them both back to Shane. 'Your pre-payment has been registered, and –' he pulled a strip of black cloth from beneath the counter '– as you requested –'

'Thank you.' Shane bound it around Emma's eyes, cutting off her most important sense, except maybe for touch. She took a deep breath as she adjusted, and could feel his closeness and warmth, reassuring her. Her body also adjusted, growing warmer and her pussy wetter as she responded to conditioning.

There was a shuffling, then Shane took gentle hold of her arm again and she allowed him to steer her forwards, around the desk. She stepped confidently, knowing that he would not lead her astray, though her ears strained until she heard the familiar buzz that meant the inner door had been unlocked from the desk. A rush of air brushed her face as the door opened, and Shane guided her through.

The tenor of the place immediately changed. Perhaps it was only because she knew, but she felt as if she could sense the dimness of the dungeon as they stepped over the threshold, though she couldn't see it through the blindfold. The air felt chillier in here, and the noise was unmistakable. Somewhere, something cracked against fragile flesh, and someone screamed in a mix of pain and pleasure. Low conversations buzzed, moans echoed, and the slap of flesh against flesh was a constant soundtrack in the background of this lurid place. Her whole body flushed with heat even as goosebumps broke out on her bare arms.

They moved through the club, twisting and turning as he took her out of the main room, and eventually she heard the rattle of a locker, the shifting of cloth and finally the slam of the locker door before he took her arm again. For a small fee, any member in good standing could rent a locker to store toys and clothes for use at the dungeon, and circumvent any embarrassing transportation issues.

'Through here,' her Master said in a low voice. He guided her through a final door and shut it behind them, then took the hem of her shirt and pulled it up without warning. She raised her arms quickly, allowing him to undress her. 'You have glorious breasts,' he told her, spilling them free of her bra. He cupped them in his hands, his fingers hot and rough as he grabbed and squeezed, massaging and manipulating them with pleasure. It was the kind of gentle roughness that she had always had trouble convincing boyfriends to offer. The kind of touch that made her melt with pure desire.

Emma sighed and stepped forward, leaning into his touch and begging wordlessly for more, but Shane pinched her nipples, hard, and she stopped. 'Girl,' he said.

'Yes, Master?'

'Don't distract me. We've got to get you properly dressed.'

'Yes, Master.' Properly dressed could mean anything, here. Some Masters paraded their subs around naked or nearly so. Some preferred their subs all wrapped up in PVC or leather. Sometimes costumes, like steampunk, appeared, and on theme nights things could get incredible. So far her Master had allowed her her modesty, but as her submission to him grew, she had come to realise that she would willingly give him more.

But perhaps not today. He peeled away her pants and panties, inhaling deeply as her fragrant sex was exposed, but he only paused for a moment to run his fingers through the slick wetness there before he shifted and tapped her foot, requiring her to lift it. She placed a hand on his shoulder so that he could slide a smooth stocking over her foot and unfurl it up her leg. It ended at her thigh, and he traced his finger the rest of the way up to her pussy for another sweet swipe through her wetness before he pulled away again.

'No belt, Master?' she asked, confused.

'We're not done yet,' he said. 'I have something else in mind for you tonight.' He rolled the other stocking up her leg, startling her with a quick flick of his tongue against her clit before he stood again. 'I'm looking forward to fucking you tonight,' he said, his voice dropping. 'I'm going to spread those black-clad legs wide open and use that slimy cunt.'

'Yes, Master,' she whispered. Already she could feel a trickle of moisture escape her swollen lips as her body responded to the promise in his words. She barely noticed as he slid fabric over her head and pulled it down, settling a skirt low on her hips. Would it be here in the dressing room? No, probably not. He would draw out the pleasure, teasing her and torturing her before he took her.

'I have a present for you, Girl.'

'Thank you, Master.'

'You thank me before you know what it is?'

'I'm grateful for anything you give me, Master,' she replied. She meant it. He'd taken a chance on her and taught her submission, and there was nothing he could give her that would displease her, because it would mean he'd been thinking of her.

She could feel the smile in his voice as he answered. 'Then lift your arms up.'

When she did, she felt something close around her body, soft as silk but stiff and constricting as he fastened it along the front of her body.

'Turn around, now,' he instructed, and she did. His touch at her back was the only notice she got before she was nearly pulled off her feet, and he delivered a swat in reproof. 'Brace yourself, Girl.'

'Yes, Master,' she said, but the words came out on a squeak as he pulled again and she felt the garment tighten against her ribs.

'You're wearing your first corset,' he said conversationally. She tried to gasp again, but he yanked at something in the middle of her back and she felt the air driven out of her instead. 'Shallow breaths, Girl. Don't panic, or you'll faint.'

She wasn't sure she had the breath to answer, so she hoped he would accept the nod she offered instead. He continued to tug and tighten, and she felt her body contract as the constriction moved from the top of her ribs down to her waist, and then again from her hips up to that centre point where her narrow waist was shrinking.

He gave one last great tug and then tied a knot at her back, and Emma felt herself sway. Her breath could come only in shallow pants as she tried to breathe without expanding her ribs. But air wasn't the only reason she was swaying on her feet. Oh, God! The constriction! The bondage! She felt wrapped up and constrained, and her body swam with pleasure, arousal and a sense of submission as she dropped deep into subspace at the sensation.

'Oooh,' her Master cooed, 'I'd hoped you would react like this. That's right, my beauty, feel me crushing you.'

She found enough air to whimper, still swaying on her feet, and her Master laughed in delight. 'I suppose it would be better to forgo the heels tonight,' he said. He settled something light on her back and brought cords around to tie in front of each arm, though she barely noticed, focused as she was on the erotic crush of the corset.

He reached into the front of it to adjust her breasts to his satisfaction, his fingers pinching and teasing her as he shifted her body around to please him, then he settled something on top of the blindfold and she heard his feet scuff the floor as he stepped back.

'Perfect. Now, you just stand there and look sexy for me while I change,' he said. She was glad to comply, since she wasn't sure she could do much else even if he'd asked it of her.

A minute later, she felt him approach her again. 'I was going to make you leave your blindfold on tonight, but you're just too gorgeous to resist. I want you to see how enchanting you look.'

She barely had time to reflect on his unusual word

choice before the strip of black cloth was pulled out from under the mask that rested on her face, and she stared at her own image in a full-length mirror.

'My God ...' The corset was silver and black, and made her waist into a tiny wisp that seemed barely there, tucking her in and spilling out above, giving her breasts a shelf on which to rest and be displayed. They bubbled up under her chin, impossible globes of perfectly rounded flesh, like peaches waiting to be bitten into. Below, she was more exposed than she had expected. Her black lace stockings were clipped to garter hooks on the bottom of the corset, and her pussy was terribly exposed beneath a sheer silver skirt that glistened like a waterfall and concealed nothing. The weight on her back had been a magnificent pair of white, black and silver fairy wings, tied on with ribbons, and a shining silver mask hid her eyes and nose.

The cumulative effect was of a shining silver fairy – some ethereal creature captured in her form.

'Master ...'

'It took me for ever to get all of the pieces,' he said, pleasure suffusing his tone. 'It had to be perfect.'

'It is. It's perfect. Oh, Master ... it's beautiful.'

'You're beautiful,' he corrected. 'Now, come on and let's have a bit of fun.'

She shuddered, realising for the first time that he was going to lead her out of here with her pussy bared for all to see, but she steeled herself to make a good showing and to make her Master proud. If he wanted others to see his property, then she would make sure they saw something he would be pleased with.

It was a new concept, and she turned it over and tasted it as he wrapped a long, fine silver chain around her neck to use like a leash. She wanted to please the man she chose to submit to. He wanted her to display herself. So she wanted it too. The thought was sweet and spicy on her tongue, like cinnamon sugar.

He tugged gently on the leash, and she put her chin up, her posture already perfect from the corset's embrace, and followed him through the door. She was stunned again when she saw how the rest of the clubgoers were dressed. Fairy wings and masks abounded, and many of the women and a few of the men wore clothes as ethereal and revealing as her own, though nothing was quite so regal or so beautiful. She forgot, for a moment, that she was supposed to be putting on a beautiful display, and simply stared around her.

So she was surprised when her Master stopped in the middle of the room. She turned to him, waiting for her next direction, but he just smiled at her and waited. Was she supposed to kneel? She hesitated, uncertain, until a clinking sound drew her attention and she looked up. A large hook was descending from the ceiling right next to her.

Cold chills passed over her skin as she realised that it was meant for her. Here? In the centre of the room? Her breath came faster and shorter, and again she feared that the corset might make her faint. Everyone seemed to have stopped what they were doing to watch her Master and her, and her eyes went wide. 'Master?'

'Hands, Girl.'

She gave him her hands without thought, and a little warmth stole back into her as she obeyed his command. He had a pair of leather cuffs in his hand, which he must have pulled from the toy bag at his feet. She'd never seen them before, but they were gorgeous – narrow and black, each with a chain around the outside as a small decorative element, emphasising their purpose.

Shane fastened the cuffs around each of her wrists, then pulled a small padlock out of his pocket, checked the key and snapped the lock through the clasp of both cuffs. They wouldn't come off again without the key, and she couldn't pull her wrists apart more than an inch or so. It was plenty of space to slip the hook into, however, and Shane did so. He gestured, and someone on the edge of the room lifted the winch until she had to stand on the balls of her feet, her body stretched at full extension.

'Are you comfortable, Girl?'

'Not really, Master,' she answered honestly. Her legs would quickly tire, and she could barely breathe.

Shane laughed. 'That's all right, you look wonderful.

Like you're about to take flight. Doesn't she look gorgeous?'

A murmur of agreement went up from the dozen or so people standing around her, and she felt a flush flow through her, spreading across her face and down beneath her corset like spilled wine.

'Are you aroused, Girl?'

'Yes, Master,' she whispered. It was true. Her body responded to the humiliation the way a man responded to porn, and her thighs were sticky with her arousal.

He gathered up her skirt in front of her and reached between her legs, his eyes on hers. 'Let's just see.' His fingers came back shining and slick, and he held them up for his audience to admire, then he held them to his nose for a deep breath, and wiped his fingers clean on her breasts. 'You smell like a slut, Girl,' he said. She whimpered as her pussy contracted in pure, aroused desire.

Then he turned away from her, and she sagged in her chains as he withdrew the electricity of his attention. 'Suggestions?'

'Spank her!'

'Cane her thighs!'

'Redden those tits!'

He allowed the crowd to shout their suggestions for a moment, running over each other in a wave as they determined how she would be tortured for her Master's and their pleasure. She squeezed her eyes shut, but nothing could shut out the terrible, erotic knowledge that she was on display, and for public consumption tonight.

The room suddenly silenced, and she opened her eyes to see Shane drop the hand he had raised, then bend to dig through the toy bag.

'I like the idea of pleasure as pain, tonight,' he said. He had pulled out the vibrator. The big one. Oh, God.

Emma felt a new flood of moisture down her legs as her body prepared for the intense pleasure that awaited her, and her Master smiled as if he could smell her readiness. Maybe he could.

He lifted the front of her skirt and tucked it decoratively into the corset so that it was open in the front and draped beautifully on either side in shimmering waves. She tried to control her breath, knowing that letting herself pant with desire as she wanted would take her breath away.

'Are you ready?'

'I don't know.'

'Trust me.'

'Always.' He met her eyes and held them, and she stared into his depths as the buzzing began. The contact broke a moment later when the harsh vibrations broke over her clit, shocking her with the sudden rush of pleasure. She cried out and threw her head back, counting on her bonds to catch her as her body went rigid and spun out of her control; her entire focus was now on that one small point of pleasure as it grew ... grew ...

Shane had timed it before; it had never taken more than two minutes for her to come with this toy, aroused or not. She couldn't tell how much time had passed tonight, but she supposed it was no different. The pleasure flooded her, fierce and insistent and nothing like the natural, grinding pleasure of sex. And when it broke, it broke like a bolt of electricity, straight to her clit, making her convulse and scream with the concentrated shock of pleasure.

He gave her only a moment to regain her small, gasping breath before he applied the buzzing toy again, and this time it ached as it drove her harshly towards that jagged edge. She gasped as much as she could and fought it, but she could barely move and there was no escape except to fall ... fall ... She managed, somehow, to draw enough breath to scream, and this time the humming assault didn't stop. Her body clenched and tightened and her eyes pressed shut as light flashed behind her lids. The pleasure was already driving into pain, and her body trembled with the effort to stand, with the need for more air, with the passion and endorphins, with the urge to escape.

A voice was whimpering and crying out, high and breathy, and she recognised herself. The world felt as if it were tumbling her over and over, and if she didn't know better she might have thought that she was being electrocuted to death through that little contact with her clit. It was eternity. It was agony. It was pleasure beyond beating and sweetest, cloying pain.

And then it stopped.

Emma sagged in her bonds, aware for the first time of the pain in her shoulders and arms. She panted shallowly, desperate for breath, and her head spun with the remnants of the torturous, endless orgasms. Dimly, she was aware of Shane's arms around her, lifting her up to unhook her wrists from the winch without waiting for it to be lowered, and, when he set her back on her feet again, she sank slowly to her knees.

'How do you feel?' he asked, his voice quiet in the room, which seemed to have gone still with tension.

'Thank you, Master,' she said, not sure what else to say. Her head had begun to clear, but she still wavered in her pose there on the floor, unwilling or unable to trust her legs to hold her.

It took a long moment for her to gain the strength to look up at Shane. When she did, her eyes met his and his gaze was strangely vulnerable.

'This is my world,' he said. She blinked to clear her eyes and glanced around; there were still a dozen people staring at her with lust and anticipation. She blinked again, hard, and returned her attention to Shane. He had been waiting for her. 'Was tonight too much for you to handle?'

She paused, wanting to think it through before she

answered, but her words, when they came, were the only words she ever could have spoken. 'No, Master, not if it pleased you.'

He raised one hand, and she saw that he held another cuff like the pair on her wrists. An ankle cuff? Her breath caught on the corset as she tried to gasp. Not a cuff ... a collar.

'Then will you do me the honour and pleasure of wearing this?'

Her tears and the corset threatened to conspire to strangle her, so she could only nod. It was enough, though, to set off the silent crowd, who she now realised had been waiting for this moment. They exploded into motion, clapping and moving to congratulate Shane, then breaking off into pairs or small groups to return to their own erotic games.

'Now, Girl,' Shane said, drawing her attention back, 'I believe I promised to fuck you silly in that gorgeous outfit. Shall we go find a private room so I can deliver?'

She smiled, overwhelmed, and yet knowing the perfect words. 'If it pleases you, Master.'

It did.

Border Crossings
Giselle Renarde

I've read a lot of smutty stories where two strangers meet at a bar, go on to have the most mind-blowing sex of their lives, and at the end it's revealed these people aren't strangers at all – in fact, they're a happily married couple playing some kind of fantasy role-play game. I'm not going to tell you a story like that, though I very easily could. God only knows I do enough pretending in real life. This time, it's nothing but the truth.

My husband and I are very different people behind closed doors. You really wouldn't recognise us. Well, that's an exaggeration. You'd surely recognise me – I wear men's clothes most workdays anyhow, and my tits are pretty much invisible under my orange safety vest – but Gary?

Gary you wouldn't recognise in a million years, not under a long auburn wig and a thick veneer of cosmetics.

Not wearing nylons and heels and a breezy little sundress. You wouldn't recognise him ... unless, of course, he was strolling down the sidewalk holding my hand. Then it might dawn on you just what was going on. Recognition by association. And, living in a relatively small town, neither of us was willing to take that chance. We'd never left the house together, but that's not to say we didn't want to.

The moment Gary's parents invited us down to the States for a bit of cross-border shopping, I saw my husband's eyes light up. It was fireworks, the look that passed between us. We knew each other's minds too well: if we were out of town, in a different country even, nobody, but nobody, would recognise us. Finally an opportunity to go out together! He could slip a dress and some makeup and whatnot into my suitcase and who would know it wasn't mine?

Now, the trouble with buying a house you can't afford – which is just what Gary and I did – is that you don't have a red cent left over after that monthly mortgage payment. We were lucky to scrounge enough cash to pay the electricity bill, let alone put gas in the truck and food on the table. That's not to say we weren't happy, only that we wouldn't have been able to take this little vacation if it wasn't for Gary's parents driving us all down in their minivan, and then sharing their hotel room once we got there. Not exactly a second honeymoon when you've got your in-laws in the next bed, but it wasn't meant to be a romantic getaway. A quick escape from everyday life, more like. It would do us some good.

Gary's mom was a down-to-earth, matter-of-fact sort of woman, and his father the strong silent type. I'd always liked them both. Even so, when you're spending every hour of every day with another couple, no matter who they are, eventually you need your escape. More than that, Gary and I were both itching to slip into something a little more comfortable. In his case that meant women's clothes, in my case men's. The whole trip I'd been wearing femme sweaters for my in-laws' sakes. Poor Gary couldn't even get away with a little nail polish on his toes, because what if his parents caught him changing his socks? You forget how much freedom you've got until it's taken away, that's for damn sure.

I guess Gary's parents were feeling claustrophobic too, because the night they announced they had tickets for *Wicked* over at Shea's, they didn't invite us along. Instead, they were kind enough to give us a gift certificate for a swanky little restaurant down the street from our hotel. We didn't exactly plan for that night to go the way it did. The arrangement wasn't to make our separate ways to the restaurant, fall in love all over again and then fuck in the ladies' room, but I'm sure as hell glad it happened that way.

The departure delay was caused mostly by Gary. First

93

we had to wait for the in-laws to leave before we could even dream about dressing. Then, once we were sure they weren't coming back until after that curtain fell at eleven o'clock, I was racing towards the finish line. Maybe it's typical that Gary should play the tortoise, taking for ever to get shaved and made up and lotioned and potioned in the bathroom. True, there was a hell of a lot more prep work involved for him, but once I'd flattened my tits under the old pair of Spandex bike shorts I'd fashioned into a tube top, all I had to do was slip on a nice white shirt, my favourite leather vest and the bolo tie Gary's grandfather passed down to him. I wore jockey shorts under my trousers, but I didn't worry about having no bulge down there. My belly hung over my belt far enough that nobody'd be looking anyhow, and the number of times I've been taken for a man at work or wherever ... well, let's just say I wasn't concerned.

So, I was ready and waiting ... and waiting ... and waiting, and I didn't want to stress Gary out, but I was getting hungry and time was marching on. Finally, I just had to tell him, 'If this doesn't happen soon, it might not happen at all.'

'You go,' he called through the door. His voice was wispy and high. I could tell he was practising for the restaurant. 'I've still got so much to do and ... oh, fuck!'

The panic in his voice worried me. 'Are you OK?'

'I poked myself with the mascara brush.' Now he

was getting irritated. 'Look, I can't concentrate with you listening in. Go to the restaurant and I'll meet you there.'

I was a little disappointed Gary didn't want to walk over together, candy on my arm, and in truth I'd have preferred to give him a once-over before going out in public, but I didn't want to pile any more stress on his plate. Anyway, I had faith in my husband. If I didn't, how could we possibly live this way?

It felt good just stepping into the hallway, even though there was nobody out there. Getting in an elevator full of people felt even better. Nobody looked at me weirdly, or stepped away like they would if they thought I wasn't what I seemed to be. Just walking down the street, passing people who didn't care who I was, felt so empowering I strutted all the way to the restaurant.

The place was cosy and dimly lit except where they had little lamps illuminating local art. A bunch of tables were pushed together on one side of the place. All guys over there, mostly older men, maybe having a business meeting or some kind of refined stag night. When a young black woman with a gorgeous smile walked up to me, my heart raced. What if she saw through the outfit? What if my voice came out sounding too high? 'Are you closed?' I asked, feeling stupidly incoherent. 'Private party?'

'That's a private party,' she said, nodding to the men, 'but we're not closed. Table for one?' Her smile never faltered, and that made me feel like a million bucks.

'For two,' I told her. When she led me to a quaint booth away from the men, I realised there were more people here than I'd initially seen, and that put me at ease. 'We got a gift certificate from the in-laws.'

'Nice! Special occasion?'

That girl was so receptive I just wanted to pour myself into her. 'Not really. Just visiting from up north with …' I had to stifle myself before I ended up saying '… with my husband and his parents'. 'With the family.'

We're not big drinkers, but I ordered a half litre of the house red. When the girl tittered I thought the jig was up, until she apologised and said she should be used to Canadians and our metric drink orders by now. She said she'd bring a half bottle.

I tried to study the menu, but I was so nervous waiting for Gary that the words blurred before my eyes. Instead, I studied the other patrons: a well-dressed couple, three noisy young women, a sombre man eating alone. I had to shake my head when I realised anyone looking at me would see the same thing: a man alone. It felt good.

As time marched on and the girl all in black hovered, I started feeling nervous for Gary. What if he'd got himself into trouble on the way? The restaurant wasn't far from our hotel, but anything could have happened. Just because I thought my husband looked pretty damn good in a dress didn't mean everybody would. I couldn't stand the thought of somebody harming my Gary, but, just as I stood up to go searching for him, the door crept open.

It was like a black and white film, the whole entrance. A foot in a patent-leather pump slipped through the door, followed by a bare ankle, a shaved calf, a hairless knee, even a thigh. The dress was long but slit down one side. If it wasn't for the high neckline and long sleeves, he'd have looked exactly like Jessica Rabbit with that long auburn hair and the pouty red lips, false lashes, purple eye shadow. Some might have said my husband had gone overboard, but one look at him lit a fire in my belly.

I walked to him in a daze, and for some reason said, 'Hello, stranger.'

'Well, hello to you, too.' His voice was soft and I thought a few of those men at the big table might be staring, but all I could focus on was the hand he raised to my lips. I kissed it. Deep-red nail polish. Perfection. 'I see you've ordered wine and two glasses.'

Leading my rabbit to the table, I said, 'I've been waiting for a girl like you.' Oh, I'd never felt so suave in all my life. 'I'd like to buy you dinner, if you'll have me.'

'I'll accept the dinner,' Gary replied, 'but I don't know about having you. You haven't even introduced yourself, you cad.'

Well, what name was on the tip of my tongue? Of course, 'Gary.'

He pressed his full red lips together like he was trying not to laugh. 'Well, then, I guess that makes me Shawna. Very pleased to meet you, Gary.'

Nobody in that restaurant was staring more intensely than me. I was smiling so hard I thought my jaw might break. When our server came around, I could tell she was uneasy. She looked firmly at me, only offering the odd glance in my beautiful date's direction, so I ordered quickly for both of us. The last thing I wanted was for Gary to realise the girl might be on to him.

But Gary was too caught up in our shared fantasy to perceive the world as threatening, thank goodness. 'How forward of you,' he said, 'ordering for a stranger.'

'Are you so strange?' I asked.

He leaned in close, keeping his synthetic hair away from the tea light on the table. 'You have no idea.'

I leaned in, too. 'Oh, I think I do.'

We hadn't flirted like this in years. I thought my heart was going to leap out of my chest, but instead it buried itself between my legs, throbbing there, the sensation intensifying with every shared smile. If I didn't know better, I'd have sworn I had a cock and it was growing harder every time I touched Gary's fingers, or every time he winked at me. I knew I loved my husband, but it had been years since I'd felt such a desperate attraction to him ... to *her* ...

'So,' I said. 'Do you come here often?' I admit I was out of practice.

He rolled his eyes, but smiled. 'No, just visiting. I'm from Canada.'

'What a coincidence – so am I!' I upped the ante. 'I'm here with family and we're leaving tomorrow.'

'Pity,' he said, spreading a black linen napkin in his lap. 'You seem like just the type of man I'd like to get to know a little better.'

When he sipped red wine between red lips then licked the rim of the glass, my hips ached to jut forward, to ram into his ass, to fill him up. If only I'd brought a toy or two on this trip, but I didn't want to risk the in-laws finding my strap-on.

'You know, I have a feeling we were meant to cross paths.' Was I grasping at straws, or did he enjoy the game?

'I bet you say that to all the girls.'

'No, no, no. I'm an honourable man.' Oh, yeah, he was enjoying it. The glint in his eyes told me so. 'Trust me, Shawna. You're a very special lady.'

If I thought it felt strange to call my husband by my own name, it felt even stranger when he gushed, 'Why, thank you, Gary.'

Someone from the kitchen brought our coq au vin and offered a cordial bow as he bid us, 'Enjoy.' Even though I earned more money than my husband, I'd never felt like a provider until that moment – and I wasn't even paying for this meal. There was just something about the way people addressed me when I was the man at the table that made me feel … cocky …

As we ate, I gazed across at the woman I could hardly see as my husband, and I smiled. 'What?' he asked, looking down at his dress, self-conscious.

I finished chewing before I spoke. 'I've just never been so immediately attracted to anyone. Ever.'

That brought another smile to Gary's lips. 'I know exactly what you mean.'

Talking took precedence over eating, and we flirted throughout dinner, spending for ever and a day consuming our rich chicken and mushrooms and the tender egg noodles served alongside. Either the wine went to my head or the server got over her initial apprehension, because her smile seemed back in full force as she took our dessert order.

'I shouldn't,' we said both at once, then laughed in harmony.

'But we will,' I went on, gazing slyly across the table as I ordered a fondant cake. It was served with raspberries and vanilla ice cream, which melted across the plate from the heat of the chocolate. I watched my husband bring that sweetness to his painted lips, savouring chocolate, savouring vanilla. He purred. The experience of watching him eat was exquisite, and my body pulsed with a desire I worried would remain unfulfilled.

Time was not on our side. We'd started dinner behind schedule, and it was getting on. The couple, the women, the loner – everybody but the big group of men had already left. It was too late now to get back to the hotel and enjoy a prolonged roll in the hay without worrying that the in-laws might walk in at any moment. The frustration of it all burned in my chest. It wasn't often that I felt really and truly aroused any more, and I hated the idea of wasting that throbbing desire. I wanted to blame Gary for taking so long to get ready, but how could I when the result was sitting across the table, the most gorgeous sight I'd ever seen?

Worse yet, I knew we'd never get to do this again. We couldn't go out in town, and it would be years before we could afford a vacation together, just the two of us. A sublime confluence of circumstances had led us here, to this night, this moment together, and I couldn't let it go to waste. I wanted this lady in red, my husband but not my husband, and I was going to have her.

'Come with me,' I said while our server was busy with the big group. I slapped the gift certificate and a tip down on the table, grabbed Gary's wrist and pulled him through a door marked with those familiar man and woman icons.

Beyond the door was a steep set of stairs and I went down while Gary hissed, 'What are you doing?'

I didn't stop until we'd reached the bottom. 'All the

101

female patrons have gone.' There was a pleading quality to my voice, and a look in Gary's eyes to match. 'We won't get caught.'

He smiled and pushed open the door to the ladies' room. 'You want to?'

'Do you?' I locked the door. It was only one big stall anyway, and fairly dank for such a smart restaurant.

In those heels, Gary was ridiculously tall, looming high above me as he closed in. 'I should warn you ... I'm not like other girls.'

My back was up against a wall. 'That's OK, because I'm not like other guys.'

Suddenly we were kissing, and it was so hot my whole body caught the flame. I realised, as we crawled up each other's bodies, him gripping my ass, me touching the softness of his water-bra breasts, that I couldn't remember the last time we'd kissed like this. We often pecked on the lips, often kissed goodnight, but it had been so goddamn long since we'd shoved our tongues down each other's throats that I honestly couldn't recall when it had last happened. For a moment, that made me sad. Then I thought how wonderful it was to have this one night of debauchery, and my spirit soared.

Feeling my husband's thigh, I ran my hand up that Jessica Rabbit slit as I kissed my way down his neck. I didn't realise I was moaning with the pleasure of it all until he shushed me. When I pressed my face into his fake boobs, he stifled a chuckle, and I continued along a frenzied path downwards. What was I doing, exactly? Well, I hadn't planned that far into the future, but when I got there I pulled hard on the gaffe that keeps it all in place. He pushed his silky panties down after, and I tumbled to my knees to watch his parts untuck. It fascinated me, the way he managed to push his cock and everything way back up into his pelvis. Every time his balls spilled out of that unlikely hole, it looked as though they were born from a pussy. Then the head of his cock emerged, followed slowly by the shaft. I never could understand how it all fitted in there, or how he managed to shove his dick inside his body, but there it was. I'd just watched it happen in reverse.

I didn't plan on sucking my husband off in a restaurant bathroom, but as soon as his cock materialised from within his body I just had to feel it in my mouth. It usually took a lot of effort to get Gary hard, but that night was a brilliant exception. I don't know if it was the feel of the dress, the sexual tension throughout dinner or the knowledge that this all had to happen lightning-fast, but the moment his mushroom tip passed through my lips he was rock-solid. When he forced his shaft down my throat, I sputtered but recovered before he could pull out or apologise. I wasn't used to his cock getting so big. Even in my mouth, it usually only got half hard. Tonight was truly beginning to feel like an encounter with some stranger I'd never really known. This gorgeous woman with a cock was fucking my throat like rapid-fire, so fully erect I'd have gagged if I could react fast enough.

Closing my eyes, I pretended this was a glory hole and I was the guy on the receiving end. Stranger, stranger; fucker, sucker. I took it all in as that cock pummelled my throat, tasting faintly of sweat, piss and pre-come. After all, it had been shoved inside my husband's body for a while. The aroma was baked in with his body heat. It was wonderful.

I couldn't say if I felt like a man or a woman doing all this – I just felt like the best possible version of me. I wondered if Gary felt the same way as I rose to my feet and bent him over the sink. He whimpered at the loss of my mouth, until I squirted some plain white hand lotion into my palm from the bottle beside the soap dispenser. Pulling his dress out of the way with one hand, I gripped his firm dick with the other, slathering his shaft with lotion before letting him take over. I rubbed more lotion against his puckered asshole, watching his dark eyes in the mirror as I pressed my fingertip inside. His gaze was pleading, and the look was so fucking sexy I actually growled.

'You want me to fuck your ass?' I asked, my voice low and hoarse.

He whispered, 'Please, yes.'

I felt like a God as I pushed one finger inside, sensing

the familiar resistance of his ass ring against my knuckle. Those muscles were damn tight. When he clenched, I could hardly move. When he released, I shoved another finger in and he sighed like this was heaven. Maybe it was.

Even if I hadn't been able to hear the wet slap of his hand on his dick as he jerked himself off under the sink, I'd have felt the hurried motion in his arm. It turned me on in a way I'd never quite experienced. I felt like everybody upstairs in that restaurant knew just what we were doing, and they envied me. My ego was bloated, and that was incredible. Locking my gaze to his in the mirror, I pummelled his ass with two fingers, making him moan when I added in a third.

'You like that, baby?' Oh, I felt like a big man. 'You like it when I ram your ass?'

Gary cooed like a dove, letting his cheek fall onto the counter beside the sink. I could feel the motion of his hand like it was an extension of my body. He was already set to come. It usually took ages, if it happened at all. Is this really my husband? I wondered. And, in a sense, the answer was no.

With the hand that was still gripping his dress I reached down to swaddle his balls in the fabric. His lips formed a gorgeous red O like he was dying of pleasure, but he didn't make a sound. That hand I couldn't see just kept slapping away at his dick. I wanted to watch. I wanted to see everything. But I satisfied myself with the look of pure bliss on my husband's made-up face, and the sight of my fingers disappearing lightning-fast inside his hole.

His eyes clamped shut. His muscles tensed. I could feel his body in mine, and his pleasure was my gratification. This was it. Gary stamped a heeled foot down on the ground and his throat released a sound I couldn't describe if I tried. The slapping stopped down below, but I pummelled his ass in double time. I could feel the come surging out of his body in pressurised spurts and smacking the concrete wall behind the sink. We were underground here. Everything went quiet.

I knew it was sympathetic exhaustion, but I felt like my legs were going to give out on me. Collapsing on top of Gary's hot body, I breathed hard against his neck. I don't know whose heartbeat I was feeling, but it pounded inside of me. My underwear was drenched in juice, but I couldn't have been more satisfied.

'Thank you, mysterious stranger.' Gary eased us both upright, but nearly fell over when he reached down to grab his purse off the floor. He pulled up his underwear and gaffe before reaching inside to re-tuck. 'Wow ... that was once in a lifetime.'

I locked arms with him, deciding to be the strong one. 'Can I walk you to your hotel room, my darling?'

Gary chuckled demurely. 'Let's just get out of here before they call the authorities.'

We made it back before Gary's parents, and I jumped

out of my man clothes and into a pair of men's pyjamas. Didn't feel the same. Gary was still in the shower when my in-laws walked through the door. With their return, the magic dispersed and everything seemed back to normal, our space invaded, our identities locked. We might never have another night on the town or public washroom tryst, but the very recollection would be jet fuel for those long Canadian winters when all we had was each other.

Black Silk Stockings
Elizabeth Coldwell

Miranda found the video by accident. Stowing the Christmas decorations back in the loft for another year, she wobbled on the stepladder and knocked a cardboard box from the shelf. Bits of junk scattered on the bare floorboards – half-a-dozen old college textbooks, a Perspex wine cooler with a crack running down its length, a string of fairy lights in the shape of chilli peppers. And a video, in one of those boxes designed to look like a classic novel that Jack always claimed were invented purely to give middle-aged men a place to store their porn collection.

Curious to see what was lurking in the faux-leather box, Miranda opened it. 'Oh, my God!' she exclaimed, reading the label. 'So this is where you've been hiding.'

There was a pile of clothes waiting to be ironed, and potatoes to be peeled for their evening meal, but the video took precedence over all that. She slotted it into the VCR/DVD combi player in the living room and settled on the sofa with a sense of anticipation.

Fuzzy lines rolled across the screen for half a minute, before the interference gave way to a title card, rendered in University Roman. *Black Silk Stockings*. The name had seemed pretentious then, even more so now, but Jack had liked it. He claimed it suited the mood of his film, and Miranda had never argued the point.

The camera tracked, as slowly and smoothly as Jack had been able to manage, down a carpeted landing. These days, he'd achieve the shot using a Steadicam and all the other tricks of his professional trade, but as a student he'd had to do everything by hand. His ingenuity and dedication had never failed to impress her.

A door swung open, revealing a half-dressed girl lying on her front upon a rumpled bed.

For no apparent reason, the film stock cut at this point from colour to black-and-white. Jack the *auteur*, mimicking something he'd seen in one of the arty French movies he'd loved at the time, Miranda thought. That didn't interest her, nor the reasons why he'd hidden his student film away, trying to pretend it never existed. She was more caught up in the way the camera moved, almost like a caress, up the girl's black-stockinged leg. It seemed to follow the thin seam that ran, straight and true, all the way up to the smooth bare skin above her stocking top. Then higher, capturing the pert, perfect globes of her backside, peeking from beneath the edge of her black teddy. 'Voyeur or lover?' the viewer was meant to ask at that moment.

'God, I was stunning in those days ...' Miranda murmured, feeling tears of loss and nostalgia pricking at her eyes, and brought the tape to a sudden halt.

'I've got a real treat for you,' Miranda said, as she cleared away the dinner plates that evening.

'Don't tell me, apple pie and ice-cream,' Jack replied, topping up their wine glasses. He was in a good mood, having just received confirmation that one of the satellite history channels had commissioned a documentary he'd pitched to them on the Dutch resistance movement. 'Better than that, though we can have ice-cream later if you want it.'

She passed the tape in its faux-leather case over to him, loving the surprised expression on his face as he flipped the box open and recognition dawned on him.

'Where the hell did you find this?' He made as though to throw the thing back at her.

'Up in the loft. Be careful with it. It's probably a collector's item by now.'

Jack winced, no doubt experiencing a pang of old shame. 'Did you watch any of it? And, if so, is it as bad as I remember?'

'I glanced at it,' Miranda admitted. 'You shouldn't be so hard on yourself. You did get the top mark in your year for it, after all.'

'Proves how little taste my tutors had.'

It was clear that, despite his open contempt for his art-school project, beneath the surface Jack itched to look at it again, if only to remind himself how much he'd improved as a film-maker since those first tentative steps. Miranda took the box from him, picked up her wine glass and headed for the living room. 'Come on, let's watch a bit of it. I promise you it won't be that painful.'

By the time Jack joined her on the sofa, she'd cued the video up at the point where she'd left it. Pulling her husband's arm around her shoulder, settling into his embrace, she pressed 'play'. Her scantily clad bottom filled almost the whole screen.

'Now I remember why Professor Flanagan rated this film so much.' Jack grinned. 'Didn't he try to get into your knickers at the end-of-year party?'

'Yes, and I might have let him, if we hadn't been an item. He always looked like he had a huge cock in those faded corduroys.' Miranda continued to watch herself, fascinated. The camera was on her face now, blonde hair tumbling from a loose ponytail to frame her laughing features. 'Oh, Jack, what happened to me?'

'What do you mean?' Jack asked.

'Look at me. I was thin, gorgeous ...'

'You're still gorgeous, believe me.' He dropped a soft kiss on her cheek. 'I was a lucky man then, and I grow luckier every day.'

She blushed at the compliment. 'But you know what I really remember about filming that scene? The underwear wasn't even silk, nor were the stockings. It was some cheap stuff I got from one of the chain stores down the road from campus. I don't think I ever wore it again, it was so scratchy and nasty. The stockings actually laddered while I was taking them off.'

'But you made it look like silk.' Now his hand was sliding down into her top, thumb gently brushing her nipple through her bra. The soft bud peaked in response, a gentle warmth flooding Miranda's pussy. Glancing at Jack's crotch, she saw the material stretched taut across his cock where it pressed up hard, as if seeking to breach his fly.

They watched a couple more minutes before she switched the tape off. 'Remember I mentioned dessert? Why don't we take it to bed?'

Her husband's expression of surprise swiftly changed to one of lustful anticipation. He didn't ask Miranda what had prompted this deviation from their routine sex play. If he had, she'd have told him it was seeing herself as she had been, back when they'd first been together and every time they tumbled into bed was an adventure, with new positions to be tried and new places to be licked and teased and stroked. The sex they had now was never less than satisfying, but it lacked the wildness, the spontaneity of those early months together.

That was only to be expected, she supposed, as she pulled the tub of premium vanilla from the freezer. Life got in the way. You couldn't spend all day fucking when jobs and responsibilities and the real world came knocking on the door. She and Jack loved each other as much as they ever had, and they did everything they could to keep their romance alive. They made the compromises successful couples their age always did; the number of friends' marriages that had either fallen by the wayside or were limping along in an atmosphere of mutual tolerance was testimony to their own hard work and commitment to their relationship. But a part of her still wanted to be that carefree, laughing girl in Jack's film, thinking only about the next opportunity to skip lectures and head instead for bed, the next seduction, the next orgasm.

So she took the ice-cream into the bedroom and fed Jack messy spoonfuls as he slowly undressed her to her underwear. As the melting confection dribbled down her collar bone and chin, and they rolled together on the crumpled sheets, licking trails of ice-cream from each other's body, she wasn't thinking about the laundry she'd have to do the following day. Her mouth closed round the head of his cock, tasting the piquancy of salt and vanilla, and she was completely lost in the moment. Even after all these years, she never tired of the way Jack felt in her throat, hot and vibrant, or the look of adoration in his eyes when she glanced up into his face, still engulfing his shaft with her ice-cream-smeared lips.

Cuddling with Jack, after he'd come forcefully down her throat before licking her to a delicious climax, Miranda reflected on her discovery of the video. Dated and full of its own self-importance as it was, watching it had provoked them into pushing at the edges of their comfort zone for the first time in ages. Tomorrow it would be hidden away in the loft again, and their brief foray back into student recklessness would be forgotten. Or so she imagined.

They'd made plans for the coming weekend: a visit to the latest exhibition at Tate Britain, followed by dinner in a little tapas place on the South Bank. Jack had to abandon those plans at the last minute, after the BBC's legal department contacted him regarding edits that were needed before his forthcoming documentary on food additives could be screened. He promised to make it up to Miranda, voice full of genuine apology, before heading off to the edit suite. It wasn't the first time his work had got in the way of their social life, but she'd come to accept it as the price she paid for being the wife of a successful TV director.

When he returned that evening, he had a surprise

for her. Champagne, and a beautifully wrapped box bearing the name of an exclusive West London lingerie boutique. Tearing the paper off, she discovered inside a black chemise, edged with lace, a matching pair of high-cut panties and a thin, frothy suspender belt. Nestling in the bottom of the box was a packet of seamed stockings.

'Silk,' she murmured, rubbing the material of the chemise between her fingers. 'Oh, Jack, it's beautiful.'

'Put it on for me,' he urged. 'All of it. I'll pour the champagne.'

Vintage fizz and expensive lingerie. Who couldn't fail to appreciate such a romantic gesture? Miranda wondered. Yet she sensed it was leading to something, as she unhooked her bra in the en suite bathroom and pulled the chemise over her head. The garment was so short it skimmed her crotch, but she loved the way she looked in it, the lace trim partially concealing her breasts and the apex of her thighs, hinting at the promise of more. The panties were equally skimpy, leaving half her bottom cheeks bare as she pulled them up over her suspenders – always the suspenders first, for easy removal of her underwear over the cumbersome straps. As for the stockings, she discovered they too were genuine silk; a little heavier and thicker than anything she'd previously worn. With less give than the Lycra-rich tights she usually wore, they seemed to hug her legs provocatively, and it took her a good couple of minutes to get the seams straight. With their fully-fashioned heels and toes, again something she was unused to, they made her feel like some 1940s pin-up girl, about to pose for a raunchy calendar to give the troops a treat. An impulse she didn't quite understand made her slip on a pair of black high heels as a final touch.

By the time she'd finished dressing, she was reminded of the outfit she'd worn in Jack's film, but this was a much classier version. Aware she must be keeping him waiting, she couldn't resist one last slow pirouette in front of the mirror, admiring the way the stockings and heels lengthened her legs, and how the panties clung to her pussy. Already her juices were seeping into the fine silk fabric.

Hot and needy, she ran her hands up her legs, feeling the contrast between the fine mesh of the stockings and her plump white flesh above. Turning and looking at herself over her shoulder, she gazed at the stocking seams, pointing their way impudently up to the thick welts, guiding the eye to the delights waiting above them.

Stepping back into the bedroom, Miranda was greeted by the sight of Jack holding two champagne flutes. As she approached he paused in the act of holding one out to her, clearly taking in the sight of her in the new lingerie. Until now, she'd never really understood what it meant when someone was described as tongue-tied, but Jack clearly seemed to have lost the power of speech. She took the glass from his nerveless grip and sipped from it, revelling in the feel of the bubbles fizzing against her tongue.

At last, Jack recovered his voice. 'You look amazing.' He shook his head slowly, as if still not quite believing in the vision before him. 'Just perfect for what I have in mind.'

'And that might be ...?'

He didn't need to answer. His guilty glance towards the bottom of the bed told her everything. While she'd been changing, he'd been busy setting up his tripod. His digital video camera lay on the bedsheets.

'When we watched my old student film the other night, I saw so many things that were wrong with it. I thought I was the next François Truffaut, and what I was really making was a glorified pop video. But you – you were the one marvellous thing about it. Miranda, I just couldn't take my eyes off you. It was like I was falling for you all over again.

'Then I was walking past the boutique today, and that chemise was in the window. I had to get it for you. I knew you'd look fantastic in it. And the stockings – God, I never knew there could be something so magical about real silk stockings.' He paused, finally getting to the point. 'And I thought – maybe tonight we could make the film I wanted to make all those years ago. One that'll never be seen by anyone but us.'

'If you mean what I think you mean, I'm going to need

some more of this champagne first,' Miranda replied, but she didn't say no. Perhaps Jack's film had roused in him the same need as it had in her, to rediscover some of the passion that had somehow been lost to comfort and familiarity as the years had passed. Lounging back against the pillows, she let him refill her glass. For the first time she noticed he'd also been busy lighting candles that filled the room with the heady scent of jasmine.

They shared kisses between sips of champagne, desire building in a slow burn. Once Miranda's glass was empty she set it aside, ready to begin.

'OK,' Jack said. 'Lie on your front, and do your best to pretend the camera isn't here.'

She remembered him instructing her to do something very similar, so many years ago in that shabby bedroom in his student house. It was difficult not to turn and look when he murmured, 'Oh, yes ... so beautiful ...', but she discovered if she glanced to her left she could catch sight of him in the dressing-table mirror. He was playing the camera lens up the length of her stocking-clad leg, lingering on the planes of her calf and thigh, before moving towards her silk-covered crotch.

'Right, Miranda, I want you to get up on all fours.' This was new, but she did as he asked. Last time, he'd been guided by his artistic vision and his need to impress his tutors. Now, she suspected, he was giving in to a more lustful impulse.

He was close behind her, and she could only imagine what was being captured by the camera as he swept it slowly across the half-covered terrain of her backside. Could it detect the growing damp spot in her panties? The wet fabric clung to her sex lips in an intimate caress, and for a moment Miranda wished Jack's fingers were touching her there, pushing the silk up into the hot, slick cavern that was her pussy.

'OK, sweetheart, reach behind yourself and ease your panties down very slowly.'

That was easier said than done. Miranda was convinced she'd topple off the bed as she used one hand to peel down her underwear. She wanted Jack to strip her, but he was living out some fantasy of directing porn she'd never known he had until now. When the panties were down far enough to reveal her pussy from behind, Jack told her to stop.

'Touch yourself.'

The command was so direct, so horny, Miranda couldn't help but moan in response. Looking back over her shoulder before she complied with his request, she saw her husband's hand clamped round the crotch of his jeans. She'd played with herself as he watched so many times before, but never with him directing the action, telling her where to stroke, how firmly to apply the pressure, when to pull back. Following his instructions, she began to understand how a woman might get off on being told what to do, stringing out her pleasure and only being allowed to come when – or perhaps if – her partner decided she could.

This was what she'd been craving since they'd watched the video together: the rush that came from trying something she'd never done before. But just because Jack had cast her in the submissive role, it didn't mean she couldn't improvise.

Miranda beckoned him to come round and stand close to her head. Reaching out, she knocked his hand away from his cock. He seemed about to complain, until she pulled down his zip. Her fingers sought for the opening of his boxers and pulled out his thick shaft. Now his lens was focused on her hand as it slowly ascended his length, then returned to the base.

'Put that thing on the tripod,' she ordered him. 'You know I've never been a great fan of shaky camerawork.'

She took the break in proceedings as an opportunity to remove her panties entirely, leaving the suspenders to frame her pussy in front, her bare bum cheeks behind. Liking the effect, the sensation of being half-stripped, she went further, slipping one strap of the chemise off her shoulder, exposing a breast. Softer and heavier than it had been in her student days, it fitted perfectly in Jack's hand, and when he came back to the bed, he took it in his grasp and strummed the nipple with his thumb.

'Strip for me, darling,' Miranda whispered as the little

nub stood out proudly under his caress. 'Show the camera how the years have treated you.'

He looked good naked, having lost the gawkiness of his younger years and filled out his tall, rangy frame. It wasn't fair, Miranda thought, how men seemed to get better looking with age, while women were only considered beautiful when they were young and unlined. But she knew her body so much better now than she had twenty years ago; she had gradually become mistress of her own needs and responses. The orgasms she had now, with or without Jack's skilful input, were proof enough of that.

She dragged her thoughts back to contemplation of her husband's body. His clothes having been disposed of without ceremony, Miranda ran her hands over his muscled back, down to his taut round arse.

'Oh, so gorgeous – and all mine.' She squeezed his cheeks affectionately.

'Hey, when did you start directing the action?' Jack's grumble was good-natured. For all the pretence that he was shooting some kind of arty porn film and she was his compliant leading lady, nothing really mattered any longer except their lust for each other.

Miranda grinned, kicking off her heels and pointing her toe. 'The moment I thought what a great shot it would be if you were to kiss your way up my silk stockings.'

'Now that sounds like a challenge.' With that, Jack took her foot in his hands and sucked her toes into his mouth. The feeling of the moistened material against her skin had her squirming. Until now, she'd never really considered the pleasure she could get from having her feet played with, but as he swiped his tongue over her silk-clad sole in broad, flat strokes she arched her body up, overwhelmed by the sensation. When he relinquished his hold on her toes and began to plant kisses up her calf, moving towards the ticklish place at the back of her knee, she wondered if she might actually come before he got anywhere near her sex.

Urged on by her breathy moans, he moved relentlessly higher, easing her leg over his shoulder so he could nibble at the soft skin left exposed by the stocking top. On another night, she would have been happy for him to carry on licking, to make her cream around his supple tongue as he lapped at her clit, but now she wanted something more direct; the feel of their bodies joined in the most primal way.

'Please, please,' she begged, 'just fuck me.' Her need was plain, and he responded to it. No more teasing, no more delaying the moment when his dick would push up into her welcoming cunt.

Still, having proved he could follow her instructions so faithfully, giving her the sweetest pleasure, Jack now seemed to need to regain an element of control. Pinning Miranda's hands together above her head, he thrust into her. Normally, he'd inch his way in, taking his time, letting her grow used to the way his girth spread her wide, but she was so wet, so open there was no need for any of that.

'I love the way you feel round my cock,' he told her. 'Like your cunt was designed for the sole purpose of holding me tight.'

'There speaks the *auteur*.' Miranda chuckled.

'No, there speaks a very horny man who just wants to fuck his gorgeous wife's brains out.'

'So stop pontificating and do it.'

When they watched the film back later, they'd both agree the camera angle was all wrong, the shot dominated by the sight of Jack's rapidly flexing buttocks, rather than the place where his shaft plunged into his wife's slick hole, only to pull out again shining with her juice. But as he fucked her with welcome ferocity, such considerations were far beyond their thoughts. She writhed beneath him, urging him on with her movements and throaty gasps. With every stroke, he took her just a little closer to the moment where her world would dissolve in orgasm before reassembling itself, just a little brighter than before.

'Almost there,' Jack announced, sweat beading on his handsome face. They gazed into each other's eyes in the moment before his climax hit him, feeling a connection that had never gone away, not even during those times when sex inevitably took a back seat in their lives. Tonight had reinforced the bond between them, and Miranda was sure there would be many more nights like it from now on, with or without the camera to record them for posterity.

'Love you,' Jack grunted as he came.

'And I love you,' Miranda replied, feeling sharp spasms of pleasure roll through her. She rode the waves, enjoying every last ripple as they slowly faded to nothing.

Jack just about had the presence of mind to turn the camera off before pulling Miranda into the security of his arms. Within minutes she slept, a satisfied, dreamless sleep that enveloped her like pure black silk.

Walk on the Wicked Side
Heather Towne

Lorraine really discovered the power of her shapely legs and feet when she was in gym class in her final year of high school. The girls' regular instructor, Mrs Dukanitch, had broken her back in a bull-riding accident and Mr Dupont had filled in for the rest of the term as substitute.

Mr Dupont was an applied mathematics scientist by training. But after going slightly insane attempting to find the last number in Pi, he'd been reduced to teaching at a high school, following the career freefall trajectory of the old adage: those who can't, teach, and those who can't teach, teach gym.

The short, stoop-shouldered, prematurely bald and bespectacled man appeared stricken when Lorraine first pranced out of the girls' changing room in a pair of super-short white shorts, her long, lithe, sunkissed legs flashing. She was a smart girl, discerning, and even though she didn't understand the psychology of it yet, she could see the effect her legs had on the limb-struck Mr Dupont. And she used it to her advantage.

She wasn't particularly concerned about her mark in phys-ed. But she *did* need top grades in her other courses if she was to get the scholarship to the college she desired. So she let Mr Dupont hold her slender, delicately constructed ankles whenever she, and the rest of the class, did sit-ups; let him hold the rope for her whenever she climbed, her trim, mounded calves hooking around the rafter-hung rope, lean young thighs squeezing it tight; and Mr Dupont was the one who personally stretched out and rubbed her smooth, slim legs whenever she came down with one of her frequent cramps. In return, the leg-obsessed man hacked into the school's mainframe and gave Lorraine's marks a six- to eight-point boost in every subject.

She did well in college, computer science and engineering becoming her chosen career path. The fact she was surrounded by brilliant men in boys' bodies, introverts harbouring raging inner desires to be dominated and used by women (in other words, quintessential leg-men), helped her cause considerably. She moved into her first apartment in Silicon Valley shortly after graduation.

'Hi, I'm Lorraine.' She held out her hand to her new neighbour.

'M-Myron,' the small, rather effeminate-looking

twentysomething mumbled, limply gripping her hand. His hair was black and stringy, his face pale but pleasant, body girlish. 'W-Welcome to the building.'

'Thanks.' Lorraine bit her plush lower lip. 'You know, I could really use a man's help carrying in all of my boxes.' Her lustrous dark hair was sleekly pulled back in a ponytail, highlighting the fine bone structure of her face, her large violet eyes and long black lashes, her red, glossy lips. Her tall, slender, statuesque body was clothed in a plain white T-shirt and pair of grey sweatpants, scuffed sneakers on her feet.

Myron looked at her sweatpants and sneakers and said, 'Oh, yeah? I, um, would like to help out, but, uh, I've got to go to the lab, to do some work.'

Lorraine curved her lips into a smile, noting how Myron's downcast brown eyes didn't wander north of her waistline. 'On a Sunday? That's too bad. Oh, well, nice meeting you.' She slipped inside her apartment with a wave of her hand that went unnoticed.

The apartment was starkly empty except for the five suitcases containing her best, most expensive clothes. She quickly shed her plain work gear and plunged her feet and legs into a pair of sheer pantyhose, wrapped her bum and thighs up tight in a black stretch-skirt, poured her peds into a pair of black pumps. A white satin blouse was added as an afterthought.

Myron was just leaving his apartment when Lorraine

stepped back out into the hallway in her changed garb. He gaped at her, gazing with widened eyes at her sculpted legs sheathed in the sheer hose, the curved arches of her feet platformed up in the pumps. His key rattled in the door lock.

'More boxes to leg on up,' Lorraine sighed at the twitching young man. 'Guess I better put my best foot forward, though, huh?'

'H-Hold on! Let me help you!' Myron left his key in the lock and leapt over to Lorraine. 'You shouldn't have to carry all that-that heavy stuff.'

'But what about your work?'

Myron's eyes were fastened on Lorraine's golden limbs, journeying up and down. 'Huh? What work?'

He lugged all of her boxes out of the rented van and up the three flights of stairs into her new apartment, trailing eagerly, oglingly after her. Then he insisted on helping her unpack, setting up her new computer and TV and PVR, even though she was quite capable of doing that all by herself.

She told him where to put things and he excitedly complied, his eyes fixated on her legs standing tautly together or swishing seductively against one another in her hose when she walked around the apartment. His reddened ears rang with the clarion click-clacking of her two-inch heels on the hardwood floors.

It was late in the evening before Myron finally had

all of her stuff unpacked and set up just as she wanted it. 'I-I guess I'd better go,' he spluttered, not moving an inch, staring at Lorraine's shining legs and feet.

'You really *should* be rewarded for all of the help you've given me, Myron,' she murmured, strolling slowly over to the transfixed man. 'And for all of the help you're going to give me – getting a job at the company you work at.'

The company Myron worked at was the largest, most powerful computer hardware and software manufacturer in the country.

'Uh, well, you don't –'

Lorraine placed an elegant hand on Myron's bony shoulder and easily pushed him down to his knees on the floor at her feet. 'You can caress my feet and my legs, if you care to.'

Myron shot out his small, soft, damp hands and clutched Lorraine's ankles. He moaned, clinging to the hose, the shapely, intricately boned structures beneath, staring up and down Lorraine's towering legs. Sweat beaded his tall forehead and his lips trembled. Lorraine smiled down at him.

His damp hands travelled higher, sweeping upwards, fingers widening and stretching to accommodate Lorraine's mounded calves, her capped knees, her lean, firm thighs. She bit her lip as the excited caress of the man's hands on her sensitive lower limbs, and the power she wielded over him with her legs, pulsed through her body.

Myron's hands slowly slid back down the long, exquisite expanses of Lorraine's legs, fingers stroking her silky hose, the silken skin beneath, until he was smoothing his palms over the contoured arches of her feet, touching her packaged toes in the open-faced pumps. He impulsively dove his head down and pressed his lips to her feet, feverishly kissing first one, then the other, fingers covetously coiling around her ankles again.

Lorraine felt the man's hot, damp lips pour kisses all over her feet and her black leather pumps, and she thrilled with the treatment. Whereas leg-men were stunned by her lower limbs, so were her legs and feet sensitive to the caress, the kiss, the lick of a man. It was a perfect match of emotions, leg-loving men and leggy woman. Except that Lorraine had better mastery over her feelings than her footmen did theirs, and thus all of the control in the leg-driven relationship.

She slid her slender hands up off her hips and onto her breasts, and cupped the taut, tingling mounds, as Myron kissed her feet, then ran his tongue up and over one arch and the other. He looked up at her for desperate approval, and she nodded, pinching her stiffened nipples through the satin and rolling the buzzing tips between her fingers.

Myron excitedly lapped Lorraine's arches like the footdog he was, painting her crested skin through the sheer hose with his warm saliva. Then he dipped his head even lower and wagged his tongue across the set of toes sticking seductively out of Lorraine's left pump, then bounced over and swiped the rounded toes revealed in her right shoe. Lorraine murmured softly, her legs trembling slightly, her nipples straining against her fingers.

Myron flowed his tongue all over her toes, around and around the glossy-nailed tops and delightfully rounded bottoms. Lorraine playfully wiggled them on their leather platforms, in their nylon encasings, as best she could, to drive the kneeling man wild.

Myron finally jerked his reddened face back up, and the blood rushed out of his head in a torrent, but still thundered in his ears. He wound his tongue around Lorraine's right ankle, nipped at the delicate structure, the tautened tendon at the back. Then he dragged his wet, widened tongue up her bladed shinbone and around to the soft spot behind her knee, and licked up onto her quivering thigh. He pulled the pantyhose with him, too ardent to be subtle, striping Lorraine's leg with his tongue.

She shivered the length of her stems, revelling in the man's open-mouthed worship. Only when his tongue started to stray under the hem of her stretch-skirt did she tap him on the head and admonish him with her eyes. Myron quickly and obediently dropped his head back down the shapely, sculpted stretch of one leg and bobbed over to lick up the lovely length of the other.

He repeated the same rapturous process as before on the other of the erotically twinned pair, winding his tongue all around Lorraine's left ankle, eagerly lapping the towering expanse of her second leg until he reached close to the pinnacle again.

'You can ... come on my feet, Myron,' Lorraine breathed, noting the throbbing, tented condition of the front of Myron's trousers. Her own body shimmered all along its length with tingling heat, her pussy at the apex of her parted legs brimming with sensation.

Myron quickly straightened up, fumbled his hard cock out and yanked on it, clutching Lorraine's moistened left leg at the knee with his other hand. Lorraine slid her own hand down into her skirt and pantyhose and onto her pussy, and touched her clit with her fingertips. Myron whimpered and jerked and sprayed hot come onto first one leather-cradled foot, then the other, unable to control himself any longer. Lorraine shuddered silently with her own orgasm, watching the kneeling man spurt out his lust onto her feet.

Thanks to Myron, Lorraine got a job at the giant computer firm. And within a year she was up for promotion. A promotion she knew she deserved but probably wouldn't get. Her boss was an aggressive young woman who didn't like the way Lorraine had been foisted on the department she managed by the dirty old HR

Director. The woman was short and squat, thick-ankled and bandy-legged.

Lorraine had only one option: bypass her boss, strut right over the woman's head all the way to the top man in the company, Charles Featon, the eccentric founder of the firm.

'Yes, yes, what is it?'

Lorraine peeked around the plastic door and looked across the vast, sparsely furnished office at the man seated behind the huge polyurethane desk. She'd slipped past the guards with her security badge and a story about delivering a package, and had waited until Featon's personal assistant had gone to the washroom. 'I'd like to talk to you, if you have a moment ... Charles?'

The man tore his piercing blue eyes off the giant 3D computer screen and glanced at Lorraine. He was in his late forties, with thinning greyish-brown hair, a hawkish nose and wiry body. He was not unattractive and was enormously wealthy. 'I don't have time for any interrupt–'

Lorraine interrupted him, slipping inside the office and shutting the door. Her hair was swept up, glossy black coils dangling. Her face was lightly but carefully made up, red lips shining juicily, violet eyes highlighted. She was wearing a light-blue satin blouse, darker-blue thigh-high skirt, sky-blue nylon stockings and cobalt-blue four-inch spike heels.

Charles stared at her – her gleaming legs and feet – as

she strolled towards him, her hips swaying outrageously, sensuously covered limbs crossing and recrossing, leather shoes and strapped-in feet piling up one in front of the other. In the stunned silence of the huge room, the sharp click-clacking of her heels on the polished cement floor echoed loudly, the erotic whisper of her stockinged limbs clearly audible as well.

Lorraine had done her research. She knew she, and her legs, were talking to the right man. Leisurely, languorous, she closed the distance between them until she stood before him. His jaws closed with a crack, Adam's apple bobbing with a hard gulp, as she slowly sat down in one of the Formica chairs in front of his desk, elegantly folded her lower limbs, then crossed them softly one over the other.

She sat back, legs forward. 'I'd like to talk to you about my promotion.'

The man's hands squealed on the desktop as he pulled them off. He rose to his full five feet seven inches, glaring at Lorraine's crossed legs, the dangling of one leather-clad foot. 'What about "your" promotion?' he tried to demand, the abnormal squeak in his normally high-pitched voice betraying him.

Lorraine uncrossed her legs and folded them together again – a symphony of nylon, a masterpiece of feminine shapeliness. 'I want one – a big one. In exchange for ...'

She unfurled her right leg up into the air, reached out

and unfastened the upraised shoe and uncoiled the leather straps from around her ankle. She slid the heel off and let the shoe drop, along with Charles's jaw again. Then she lowered the limb, so that the tapered tip was pointing at the man, foot arched and toes bunched, leg stretching out its sculpted loveliness through the electrified air.

Charles ran around his desk and flung himself down to his knees, grabbed Lorraine's erotically proffered ped and pressed it to his burning face.

'Yes!' she hissed.

'Yeah!' he yelped.

He smeared her slightly dampened, spicily scented foot all over his face. Then the dyed-in-the-silk leg-man rained kisses down upon Lorraine's ped, running his fingers around and along her humped arch, across and along the curved hollow of her sole. He'd never seen, felt, tasted, smelled a foot so beautiful before, and he'd been trodden on by the best. He wantonly opened his mouth, stuck Lorraine's ped-tip inside and sucked on her long, slender, bulb-crowned toes in their nylon covering.

Lorraine shivered, feeling the ardent, wet-hot tug of the man on her foot all through her body, his hands sliding up and down her clenched ankle and calf. She wriggled her toes in his mouth and wiggled her skirt up, revealing the blue flower-budded garter straps that held up her stockings, the blatant fact that she was wearing no underwear. Her pussy lips glistened with the moisture of sexual triumph, just a downy tuft of black fur gracing the top of her slit.

Charles crammed more of her foot into his craven mouth, fully half, sealing his stretched lips around arch and sole and sucking, as she slid her long, red-tipped fingers onto her pussy and rubbed.

He grabbed up her other foot, lovingly unwrapped the straps of her shoe and slid her high heel off. He fondled and caressed that foot, his mouth still full and sucking on the other one. Until he popped her right ped out, tilted up her perfectly matched left ped and lapped at its sole, his urgent tongue riding the thrilling rollercoaster of Lorraine's foot-bottom.

Her feet shone with the man's saliva, the tiny woven squares of her stockings clotted with wetness. He licked the equally sensitive and shaped sole of her right foot, riding the curvaceous contours with his thrilled tongue. Lorraine playfully crinkled her soles for him and he exulted, tonguing the sexy creases both horizontally and vertically. Then he pushed her feet together side by side, crammed both pointed tips into his mouth at once and sucked on them.

The corners of his outrageously stretched mouth drooled, his cheeks bulging with foot, his shining eyes rocketing up and down the twin gleaming lengths of the stems pouring out of his mouth right before him. Lorraine felt his tongue wag back and forth across the rounded balls of her feet, the tug of his obscenely stuffed mouth on her toes and half of her peds. She pushed his head up higher with her feet buried in his mouth, bringing Charles right up onto his shaking legs. His neck craned down awkwardly to hold onto her peds with his mouth.

She pulled her feet free and lowered them to the level of his bulging crotch. She held them out like that, glistening, legs gleaming, the feet perfectly arched and pointing at the pulsating lump in the powerful man's trousers. Then she darted her feet forward and pressed her toes soft and hard into Charles's erection.

'Oh, yeah!' he groaned, buckling at the knees and thrusting his groin harder against Lorraine's planted peds.

With her deft toes she grasped the rigid outline of his cock in his trousers. Then she pumped, moving her feet up and down on either side of his engorgment, her toes clutching and caressing his shaft. He impulsively grabbed her ankles and pumped her feet faster. She shook her head and squirmed her peds free, showing him who was the boss now.

Lorraine left Charles wildly straining for a moment, his eyes begging, her feet hovering just in front of his crotch, out of reach of his hands. Then she said, 'Show me your cock. Let's see if your cock is worthy of my feet, and legs.'

He ripped the zipper down on his expensive trousers and pulled his cock out into the open.

Her violet eyes widened slightly. It *was* impressive, long and thick as her forearm, wound round with blue veins and capped by a beefy purple hood. A manly cock that measured up to a lovely lady's beautiful legs and feet. She kicked his hand away, grasped the pulsating pole with her moistened nylon peds and pumped.

'Yeah! Yeah!' he gasped.

Lorraine pistoned her luscious limbs, stroking Charles's cock with her feet. Meanwhile she rubbed her pussy, buffing her swollen clit with her fingertips. He stood there shaking, fists clenched at his sides, eyes blazing down on her clasping and caressing feet on his cock. She pumped faster, rubbing herself harder.

It was a hand and foot race to the finish, to total release, who could leg it the longest. The lean muscles rippled up and down Lorraine's lower limbs, peds furiously pumping prick, fingers polishing clit. Charles jerked, cried out. Lorraine bucked.

Semen burst out of Charles's foot-jacked cock and sprayed all the way onto Lorraine's flying hand on her cunt. She screamed and shuddered, orgasm shooting through her body. His hot semen striped her thighs and legs and feet. Her hot juices flooded her fingers.

The promotion came with a proposal – of marriage.

Together, Charles and Lorraine quickly crushed or swallowed up all of their business competitors. Thanks to his genius in developing the 'ultimate computer' that could do almost anything, control all inferior competitive computer systems. Thanks to her legwork in lobbying certain men on the Commerce Committee to set aside certain anti-trust laws.

Within three years, Lorraine and her thoroughly ankled husband had created enough worldwide wealth and power and prohibitive patents to enable her to install herself as absolute ruler, with the technology to back it up. A meeting was arranged with the President to air her demands.

Lorraine stepped out of the company helicopter onto the south lawn of the White House in a black latex skirt that hemmed just below her buttline and the top of her thighs, a pair of scarlet silk stockings that flashed brilliant and lethal in the bright sunlight. Her showcased legs seemed to go on for ever. Strapped to her feet, finally halting the breathtaking cascade of her lower limbs in glorious fashion, were a pair of five-inch-heeled, opentoed, crimson leather stilettos with silver stems, which displayed her elongated, toe-popped peds to awesome effect.

The President shakily shook her hand, his eyes glued to her striking appendages. The thoughtful, introspective intellectual was an old-school leg-man, ever since his golden glory days with the Cornell swimming and diving team. His leggy First Lady glared at Lorraine, her own slender, conservatively clothed limbs not quite measuring up.

'My husband and I want a voice in world affairs, Mr President,' Lorraine declared in the Oval Office. 'We have a list of demands that –'

'Huh?' The President tore his eyes free and glanced up at the woman's determined face. 'Oh, yes, yes, the all-powerful computer. I'm afraid that's not quite the … persuader you perceive. You see, the government has a computer genius of our own – a man so brilliant in the digital dark arts, the open range of cyberspace, that he can hack into any computer and control it. He's already done so with yours.'

Lorraine rocked back on her stilettos. 'What? Why, that's –'

'Done,' the President cut her off, his clear blue eyes roaming the erotic expanses of her red-clad legs again, with more assurance, smiling at her deliciously packaged peds. 'He's in the next room. Perhaps you'd like to meet him?'

Lorraine smiled too, regaining her composure. She stood tall on her sky-high heels, skyscraper legs tautened for action. She smoothed up her skirt and murmured, 'I'd love to meet him.'

The President ushered her into the adjoining room. A man wearing dark glasses sat in a wheelchair all by himself. His limbs were shrunken. He didn't move when the pair entered the room.

'This is Jerome Chanowski,' the President announced. 'He's blind, paralysed, completely devoid of all senses, owing to a debilitating virus he caught from a rogue mainframe. His eyes are computer screens now, his brain the hard drive.'

Lorraine's knees buckled, her legs gone weak.

'Hel-lo, Lor-raine.' A digitised voice broke the silence. A cold, emotionless, sexless voice. 'Won't you sit down, t-ake a load off your feet?'

'Dress Slutty'
Grace Moskowitz

I got a text from Randall. 'Dress slutty,' it commanded. I smiled. I dressed provocatively frequently, and I had never had to be asked or ordered to do so. I knew he liked that about me. We had embarked on several kinky adventures, and I was having a great time watching him open up to a world of possibilities he had only recently discovered.

Really, he had blossomed in the time I had known him. Since his long, mostly sexless marriage ended, he had been actively exploring and opening up his sexual life, and he was the most natural dominant I had ever met, even if the least experienced. Like me, he wasn't a part of any 'scene'; he was new to the world of kink, and I just hate the careful orchestration, the deliberateness of that kink world and its denizens. The negotiation of every sexual encounter kills off the excitement of a serendipitous meeting, where attraction bubbles over into passion and sex happens spontaneously. It might not be safe, but I've always found safety to be the opposite of sexy. Plus, I hate jargon. The only problem with my aversion to carefully planned and non-spontaneous sex, however, is that I have a strong self-preservation instinct. So my days of passionate trysts springing out of nowhere with men I'd never met before were pretty much a thing of the past – and of my imagination.

But in the eight months we had been together I had had more than enough hot sex to leave me yearning for anything left unsatisfied. We'd gone shopping together for bondage gear; we'd gone to BDSM or sex clubs, touching only each other but getting our voyeuristic and exhibitionist thrills too. We'd had sex in places where we might have been discovered by someone. We tapped each other's deepest, sometimes darkest, secret fantasies, and role-played them. Randall's public sunniness cloaked a private darkness: the most depraved long-form fantasy scenarios played behind his bright-blue eyes. We sizzled together.

As I considered the order to 'dress slutty', I wondered what he had in mind for the evening. I decided to forgo the corset and the dog collar and dress classically slutty but not especially kinky, so I chose a tight-fitting, low-plunging baby T-shirt and a skirt that was not so tight that it couldn't be slid up to waist level easily. It was a little longer than I wanted, but the judicious use of four safety pins and a little Scotch tape fixed that. I chose a bordello-red lacy bra that I had bought recently but had worn only once before. I liked it because the lace was kind of rough and abraded my nipples in a way that I loved. The bright crimson made a striking contrast to my milky breasts and the dark bruises that were visible above the cups. They were starting to fade, but I knew that tonight I'd gain some new ones. The T-shirt was snug enough for my taut nipples to poke out very visibly.

I put on a black garter belt and attached sheer stockings with seams up the back. I checked: the tops of the stockings were just visible when I sat down or if I took a long stride – nicely slutty. I debated leaving the bra's matching slut-red panties in the dresser drawer, following my mother's maxim *less is more*, but remembered how much Randall liked taking them off, rolling them down over my thighs or pulling them to the side, once or twice even tearing them right from me, so I put them on, but made sure to wear them over the stockings. High-heeled boots, much too much dark eye makeup, a slick of cocksucker-red lipstick, and I was ready to go. Where, exactly, I didn't know.

When he picked me up, Randall looked me up and down, smiling appreciatively. 'You look great,' he said enthusiastically. I smiled back. 'Where are we going?' I asked.

'Dinner,' he said. 'I got reservations at that new fusion place.'

'Do we have time before we have to go?' We always make sure we have time before we have to go. Sometimes we've missed our reservations.

'Not tonight,' he said, taking me by the arm and beginning to steer me out of the door. I stopped and turned in to him for a kiss. Just as it began to turn urgent, he broke it. 'Not yet,' he said. 'Let's go.'

The restaurant wasn't too crowded, but it was busy and noisy in the bar area and we had to shout to hear each other. Sitting at the bar thigh to thigh, I felt the bonds of desire tightening. The banter between us was light and flirtatious, but there was an undercurrent of intensity. I began to wonder what he had planned for after dinner. When we were at last led to our table, I was grateful for the comparative quiet of the dining room.

The restaurant's décor had been the subject of a newspaper article on design and had been raved over by a hipster blogger I hated but read compulsively anyway. I looked around: there was a young couple, celebrating what was probably an anniversary, seated diagonally to our right, a four-top with two couples – business partners and their wives, I thought – almost directly behind us, a single man at the table diagonally and to the upper left, and behind him a couple of men on what looked like a first date, making awkward conversation and obviously trying to subtly check each other out. The lighting was subdued but warm, making everyone gorgeous.

In the bar, my slutty attire hadn't bothered me, and in fact, I kind of liked looking like a cheap pick-up, but amidst the elegant streamlined furniture, the thick tablecloths and napkins, the blown-glass light fixtures, I felt out of place, tacky-looking and conspicuous. Surely Randall hadn't meant me to look this slutty, or he hadn't realised how nice this place was. I felt hot and embarrassed, certain that everyone was staring at me, taking my measure and summing me up as the cheaply hired escort of an out-of-town businessman on an expense account.

But Randall appeared unconcerned and unselfconscious, and a surreptitious glance around reassured me that everyone was focused on his or her own dinner companions. No one was looking at me.

Except the solo diner at my eleven o'clock: he was looking right at me, eyeing me none too subtly. I looked away, embarrassed, and when I glanced covertly at him a moment later I was relieved to see him looking elsewhere.

We drank a lot of wine with dinner, and I was feeling pleasantly floaty but not drunk, when Randall said, in a voice I'd heard many times but didn't expect to hear at a nice restaurant, 'Touch yourself. Make your nipples hard.'

'What?' I wasn't sure I'd heard him correctly. We'd had sex in public places before, but those places had either been deserted temporarily, with the threat – and

146

thrill – that we might be discovered hanging over us, or sex clubs, where people go expressly to see and be seen fucking. This was different, though. This wasn't a place where we might be caught; this was a place where getting caught was guaranteed. And, unlike the sex clubs, people here didn't necessarily want to watch their neighbours.

When I looked around selfconsciously, I was relieved to notice that the young anniversary couple had left, the first-daters were completely absorbed by each other, and the foursome was engaged in a loud, drunken-sounding conversation about the national debt. The single man, however, was conspicuously looking at us – at me – with interest. It was pretty clear he'd heard Randall speak.

I hesitated, not knowing how I should react. Maybe I should pretend not to have heard or to have understood the request. Maybe I should pretend he meant it as some sort of not-funny joke. Maybe he *did* mean it as a joke.

As if reading my mind, Randall said, the edge in his voice razor-sharp, 'I told you to touch yourself. Touch your tits. Now.' My clit jumped at the tone. I realised that my boyfriend knew perfectly well that I was being watched by a handsome stranger, and that he wanted me to put on a bit of a show.

Casually, in a way I hoped would look accidental if seen by an onlooker, I brushed my wrist against my breast. Pretending to be rubbing my nose, I rubbed my forearm back and forth lightly. 'Good. Now more,'

Randall ordered. Refusing to look at the man facing me at the next table, I rubbed my palm over my nipple, feeling it harden in response. Randall made a soft noise of appreciation and I saw that, rather than looking at me, he was looking with great interest at our neighbour, who was in turn looking with great interest at my tits, whose hard nipples were getting harder under his gaze. I blushed with humiliation and excitement, and was aware that I could now smell my pussy, growing damp with arousal.

'Time to go,' Randall said, to my relief. When he came around to escort me out of the restaurant, he slid his hand, knifelike, up my leg momentarily to feel the heat coming from my cunt. I looked around nervously, but everyone except our lone spectator was still preoccupied. Still, he made no attempt to hide the fact that he was staring, and I felt the thrill of exhibitionism add itself to my arousal. Having a witness to transgression made the act of public groping even more exciting. I met the stranger's gaze and held it. As we walked past the table of four, Randall moved his hand from around my waist down to my ass, cupped a cheek and squeezed it. This time, the move was noticed by the entire table, the women glaring with hatred at both my boyfriend and me, their husbands looking at me with lust and at him with envy. Their looks freed me from my embarrassment and fear of being seen. I was past that. Good, I thought. Let them know. Let them think about what we'll be doing when we get back to my house. I hope they come later, thinking about it. I felt, rather than heard or saw, the presence of someone right behind us. It was the stranger.

He stayed just behind us as we left the restaurant, and followed closely through the parking lot as we made our way to the car. 'That guy is following us,' I murmured under my breath.

'I know,' answered Randall. 'What would you do if I told you to turn around and kiss him?' My steps faltered as my heart skipped a beat. Would he really tell me to do that? I'd never yet not complied with anything he'd demanded of me, but he'd never told me to kiss a stranger before.

'Do you mean that? Do you want me to?' From the man's attentive stares, I didn't think that such a kiss, surprising as it might be, would be unwelcome. I took an inward inventory: the man was good looking, more conventionally handsome than Randall, and a good twenty years younger than him. Younger than me, too. Would I mind? No, I realised, I would not mind at all. In fact, the thought made me suddenly very wet. Was it the idea of kissing the stranger that was so exciting, or the idea that the decision to do so had been made by Randall and not me?

My boyfriend chuckled deep in his throat as he tightened his grip on my waist, then said, 'Not this time,' and I felt an odd frisson of disappointment. 'But you want to,' he noted, and I could only agree. 'Slut,' he said, approvingly and audibly. Knowing that the object of our conjecture could hear him made me wetter still.

Randall drove onto the freeway, one hand casually, proprietarily resting on my left thigh. I reached over and stroked his cock, which bulged in his trousers, getting harder by the minute. He smiled at me. 'What would you have done if I *had* told you to kiss that guy?' he asked. 'Kissed him,' I answered. I didn't know if I really would have, but it was a hot fantasy to talk out with Randall, and I could tell that it turned him on to think of it.

We approached the exit to his apartment and Randall took it. 'I thought we'd go back to my house,' he explained. So the slutty dressing had just been for the benefit of showing me off to the diners; that was fine with me. Back at his apartment, I started for the bedroom, but Randall stopped me in the living room with a hungry kiss. I melted against him, feeling his warm, wet tongue in my mouth, his hands making their way to my nipples, pinching, twisting. I moaned and pressed harder against him. The pleasant sensation of the kiss, meeting the small jolt of pain his fingers sent to my nipples, was making me wet. He kissed me more urgently, and I could feel his cock hard against my thigh. 'You know how turned on I get when I hurt you while I'm kissing you,' he murmured as he feather-kissed my sensitive neck and simultaneously tugged almost brutally on my nipple. My knees buckled.

I wanted to squeeze his small, tight ass, or to unzip his fly and stroke his balls, but he reached for a pair of cuffs he had stashed on a shelf and cuffed my hands together behind my back. Then, standing behind me, he kissed the back and sides of my neck, slid his hands down over my straining breasts, and moved to the shortened hem of my skirt, which he pushed up to my waist. I ground my ass against him, moving it up and down over his still trousered cock.

His fingers were finding their way to my sopping slit when the knocking at the door sounded: three knocks followed a beat later by four more. I froze, feeling absurdly caught, a child discovered in an act of naughtiness. I held my breath, willing the intruder to go away, when, to my shock, Randall called out, 'Come in.'

I stood helpless, my skirt pushed up, hands immobilised behind me, unable to pull the skirt down and hide my steaming pussy that was only just covered by a rapidly dampening narrow strip of red satin. As I began to hiss, 'Randall, what the hell are –', the door opened and the stranger from the restaurant entered. My brain scrambled; I couldn't take it in. What? Who? Above all, how?

Randall didn't seem at all confused, and neither did the man, who looked at him for – what exactly? Approval? Confirmation? Both, it seemed. Randall lost no time in giving them both to him. 'Kiss her,' he commanded, if it could really be called a command when someone so clearly wanted to perform the action. The stranger walked over to me and began kissing my neck. Despite my confusion and embarrassment, my body responded. A moan escaped my lips as he nuzzled and then licked my neck. I looked over his bent head to see Randall watching with approval. 'Lena, this is Chip,' he said, when the man stopped and straightened. 'Chip, Lena. She's my little slut, and I promise you she'll do anything I say.'

I met Randall's eyes, and realised that, whatever was happening, it was no accident. This had all been carefully orchestrated: the seating at the restaurant, the orders to me there, the timing, all of it. Even my positioning when the man gave his signal knock: me facing the door, hands pinned behind my back, pussy practically exposed. I held Randall's gaze and he read acquiescence in mine – and something more than acquiescence: excitement. I didn't know who this Chip guy was, but obviously Randall did. This had all the excitement of a random meeting, but here we were in Randall's apartment: him, me and a stranger who wasn't. He was hot, and moreover so was the situation.

Randall took me by the elbow and led me to the bedroom; Chip followed. We stood by the bed, a triangle. 'I found Chip on Craigslist,' Randall said. 'I put an ad up, he answered, we exchanged a few messages, and then we met in person. I told him all about you. But if you don't want to do this, just tell us.'

I recognised the tone in Randall's voice: 'I'm going to ask you once, and then not again,' he'd say. 'Is this too tight?' Then he'd pull on the ropes binding me and they'd be almost too tight. But I'd shake my head, no, and, true to his word, he wouldn't ask again.

As with those times, I answered wordlessly this time, just holding Randall's gaze, shifting my eyes to Chip's and then back to Randall's. I didn't utter a sound, but that meant I didn't say no. 'OK,' Randall said, uncuffing me. To Chip he said, 'She's yours to do whatever you want with, except her ass. That's mine.' I couldn't help smiling just a bit at hearing that. How many times had I got wet reading an email from Randall, sent on the morning of the evening we had a date, that said simply: 'Clean yourself well. I'm fucking your ass tonight.'

'Sure,' said the guy, and Randall said, 'Let me get you a drink.' He left the room and I was alone with Chip. Chip, I thought. That's a fake name if ever I've heard one. Close up, I saw he looked even younger than I had thought before, maybe no more than his late twenties. A chip should be something small, but Chip had to be at least six feet three and built on massive lines. His arms were sturdy and thick, his legs like tree trunks, his chest a barrel. He didn't have the kind of body that hours in a gym buy you, but the kind that was factory-issued, then enhanced by a job in construction. I'm not a delicate girl, but next to Chip I felt fragile, petite.

Nor did Chip look chipper. His hair and eyes were dark, his overall appearance dour. He was handsome in a glowering way, and everything about him looked dangerous. He was as different from Randall as night was from day: you would never guess Randall's sexual persona from his public demeanour. Although he didn't tower over me and wasn't powerfully built, Randall had established total control over me. This guy could snap me in half if he wanted, and I knew I had to depend on the negotiations already conducted between him and Randall to assure my safety.

'Next to you, I feel like a –' I started.

'– little girl,' he finished. Then he leaned down and said softly, in a half whisper, 'I'm gonna fuck you like a little girl.' My heart throbbed in my clit.

Randall returned with drinks for all of us, and we toasted each other, the men conspiratorially, me a touch nervously. Then Chip took a step towards me and closed the gap between us. Holding my head between his hands, he kissed me – slowly, softly, sweetly. I relaxed into the kiss, into him, and he pressed closer against me, continuing to push, scissoring his leg between mine to steer me backwards, until I was against a wall. I opened my mouth and his tongue came in, probing and tasting. Our kissing grew deeper as our mutual need rose. He reached for my breasts; I reached for his fly.

I unzipped his trousers and pulled his cock out. It was

thick, wider than Randall's, not especially long, but promisingly hefty. I dropped to my knees and began to lick him explanatorily. 'Mmm,' he purred, and, encouraged, I closed my mouth over his shaft and swirled around and over him with my tongue. He tasted musky, salty; I could taste more pre-come than I was used to with Randall. I savoured it. Chip's hands dropped to my nipples and he brushed them with the flat of his hands the way I liked. I wondered momentarily if Randall had briefed him on how to touch my nipples. There is an electric current that runs straight from them to my clit and I have been known to come just from having my nipples sucked. But I didn't want to get carried away by my own responses, I wanted to get better acquainted with the tool in my mouth, so I put renewed energy into sucking Chip's cock.

I continued to swirl my tongue over and around his head and shaft, concentrating on the sensitive underside. Chip took my stiffening nipples between his thumb and forefinger and I moaned, sending sonic vibrations all along his rigid prick. I felt him grow harder still within my mouth as I began to bob my head up and down on him, keeping the suction as tight as I could. I cupped his balls in one hand, wrapping the other around the base of his cock. I thought about taking him deeper, but his cock had too much girth to fit comfortably and anyway, I wanted this blowjob to be more an *hors d'oeuvre* than the main course.

It had been a while since I had actually sucked a cock, as opposed to having my face fucked, and I was enjoying it. Not that I don't love having my throat fucked: I like being stripped of all agency, becoming no longer a woman giving a blowjob but a hole whose purpose is to be filled by a cock. I love the quick rush of fear that courses through me when a blowjob turns into a face-fuck. I thrill to the sense that I'm spiralling down, out of my own control and under someone else's. But now I loved the chance to savour and explore Chip's cock, to see what his response was when I changed tempos or stopped sucking and treated the length of his cock to feathery licks, only to plunge my hot mouth down onto it again. I pulled myself off him and rested his cock against the side of my cheek.

Then I rose to my feet, and looked up to see Randall watching, his cock in his hand. Chip pulled my T-shirt off over my head and pushed my bra up so that it bunched around my neck like some weird necklace. He bent down and began to kiss my breasts, cupping them in his hands. The pink nipples grew darker as they grew harder. I moaned and sighed, and Chip's touch grew less tentative.

'Bad girl,' he said. 'You're a bad girl. Aren't you?'

I nodded. 'Yes,' I breathed, 'I'm a bad girl.'

'Do you know what happens to bad girls?' he asked, and I hesitated, unsure what he thought the answer should be. I knew what Randall would have thought a bad girl deserved. I knew a bad girl would be spanked with a hand, paddled with a wooden spoon or paddle, sometimes whipped with a riding crop, until she cried, the tears running down her face to match the juices running from her pussy down her thighs. Randall would spank me and it would hurt like crazy, until suddenly I would realise that I wanted nothing more than to be fucked and that in spite of the pain – or maybe *because*of the pain – I was more aroused than I had ever been before. Then I would know that I *was* a bad girl, because only a really bad girl would like to be spanked like that, only a dirty slut would respond to a spanking by pleading to be fucked, please. *Please.*

'What?' I asked.

'They get what they deserve,' he said. 'They get fucked.' He looked at Randall for confirmation; Randall nodded.

'Oh,' I said, 'yeah.' No mention of pain, no talk of punishment. It had been a long time since my sex had come to me this purely, but I found the idea of the straightfor-ward sex Chip promised incredibly hot. I didn't need the added thrills of pain, humiliation or submission; the thrill was in the fact that I had no idea who was going to be fucking me in a few minutes and I would have had no part in choosing him. Randall had done that for me, to me, taking control away. My cunt clenched, my clit throbbed, my panties were suddenly flooded. 'Yeah,' I answered, 'I want that. I want you to fuck me. Will you fuck me?'

'Take off your clothes, Bad Girl,' Chip said, shucking his own. I got a clear view of his muscled torso, his solid thighs, his thick cock with its extra-flared head, shiny with pre-come and not yet dried saliva. I took my boots off, unzipped my skirt and stepped out of it, untangled my bra from around my throat. Before I could undress further, Chip stopped me, kissed me and nudged me towards the bed. I lay back on the side of the bed with my feet resting on the floor, and Randall came around so that he had a prime viewing angle. Chip knelt between my legs, hooked the waistband of my panties in his thumbs and pulled them tight up against me so that the gusset parted my lips and stretched tight over my budded clit, which stood out against it like a hard cock outlined by a tight pair of jeans. With his finger he traced the small bulge before peeling my sodden panties down my legs. When my bare pussy was exposed, he exhaled loudly. 'I like the way your snatch is framed by the stockings and garters,' he said. 'Leave them on.'

He bent down and kissed the inside of my thighs, working slowly up until he got to the hollow where my legs met my crotch. He licked until I squirmed, trying to get him closer to my clit. His tongue traced patterns all around it as I pumped my hips, imploring word-lessly for more contact. 'Why'd you shave your pussy, Bad Girl, huh? Was it to make it easier for a stranger to eat it?' I could only moan and sigh in response. 'Oh, yeah, you are a bad little girl,' he repeated, and used the heel of one hand to press down hard on my lower abdomen, pushing my clit up, while two fingers of his other hand slid inside my dripping hole, and his thumb flicked across my swollen button. A deep, guttural moan escaped me. It felt so good. His fingers were thick, and he beckoned me to him from inside my pussy, over and over, pumping them as he stroked. The combination of sensations conspired to make me come, gushing. He lifted my split to his mouth with the two fingers deep inside me, and, when he bent his head to dine on me, his eyes glowed. 'Come on my tongue, Little Girl,' he breathed, before bending his mouth to my pussy. Breathless from the orgasm that hadn't yet subsided, I easily complied with this demand. When he lifted his face off me, it was wet with my come, which he licked all over the outside of my mouth, then into it. My smell clung to him, deep and velvety, not as tangy and sharp as it was before I'd come. I liked the fragrance, the scent of satisfied desire. But the desire had only been partly satisfied.

'You want this fat cock?' Chip asked, stroking it. 'You want it, Little Girl?' I nodded. I wanted to be filled with his thick cock, wanted it like I had never wanted anything before.

'Good,' Chip said, "cause I need to fuck you now.' And I heard the neediness in his voice. He grabbed one knee in each hand, split me apart and slowly inserted himself into my core. He filled me so completely it almost hurt at first. I could feel my cunt close itself around him tight. He fucked slowly, almost languidly, taking his time as he pulled out, re-entering half-inch by agonisingly slow half-inch. Each time, each direction, his shaft teased my clit along the way, drawing back over it and making me desperate for more contact, longer and harder. Each time he settled all the way inside me, his balls smacking up against my spread lips, I felt fully filled up – for about one second – before I wanted to be filled even more, take him even deeper.

He fucked me frustratingly, maddeningly slowly. It was intense and deep and it made me crazy for a more direct touch. 'Fuck me harder,' I moaned. His pace didn't alter. Gave no evidence he'd even heard me. 'Please,' I pleaded. Most men don't need to be begged.

And this is where Chip proved himself.

'No,' he replied coolly, even though, mere moments before, I'd heard his breathing pick up. Even though his body was beginning to shine with a fine layer of sweat, and I could feel my own temperature rising in response. 'I like it just like this.' He looked dark and menacing, and I realised that his refusal to give me what I wanted was just a different way of establishing control.

The fucking bastard, the sadist, the … genius.

My whole body began to try and find a way to get what it craved but was being denied. My fingers dug into his ass, trying to push him deeper into me; I tried to speed up the tempo, but I was crushed beneath him, subject to his pacing.

He remained impassive, stoically thrusting into me slowly. My moans rose in pitch, frustration making me feel like a fifteen-year-old boy: the slightest touch was guaranteed to make me come like a roman candle. The more he denied me, the more aroused I got, until I was sure I was going to explode and I didn't think I could hold out much longer.

'Please,' I wailed, 'I need to come. Let me come.'

In response, Chip withdrew himself completely and handed me my vibrator. 'Let me see you come, you Bad Girl,' he ordered, replacing my pussy with his fist wrapped around himself. Practically the moment the vibrator touched my swollen, throbbing clit, I came. It was the kind of orgasm that comes along rarely, ripping a scream from my throat. This brought an answering groan from Chip, whose fist moved in a blur until he rained come all over my tits and belly, decorating them as if he were using a power hose to deliver that sweet glazing to a pastry. He redirected his stream, and my face caught the last salty drops.

Now Randall moved in, licking another man's come from my body and feeding it to me from his tongue. Without a doubt, I'd never been part of a sexier moment than this. Chip moved over to make room for him, and

Randall attacked me with all the force of a starving man who's been forced to watch a stranger eat a steak before he finally gets served.

Randall held my hands above my head, so that my throat and breasts were displayed, making me feel beautiful and vulnerable. He growled hungrily and sank his teeth into the lower slope of my left breast, biting and sucking as ferociously as any sexy *True Blood* vampire. I moaned and thrust my breast more urgently up to his rapacious mouth. He was marking me, claiming his territory with more than his customary ferocity, and I knew that deep-purple bruises and rings of bite marks were already beginning to blossom on my breasts.

I was still clutching my dildo-vibrator, and Randall told Chip to take it from me and to thrust it up inside me. Chip did and I noticed he was hard again, or maybe he'd never gone soft. He fucked me with it, while the vibrating part buzzed my clit, the stimulation moving on and off as Chip worked the dildo in and out. Then Randall told Chip to let me control it, and let go of my hands. I instantly pressed the dildo all the way home and left it there, moving up and down on it, so my clit got the full sensations.

'Turn over,' Randall rasped, and I complied as gracefully as I could, rolling onto my stomach with the vibrator/dildo still in place. I didn't know if I was going to get spanked or ass-fucked, and my body trembled with anticipation mixed with just a little fear at the thought of either. But there was no way that Randall could hold out for the duration of a spanking any longer. His control seemed to have fallen away as he watched Chip fuck me. With one hand on the back of my neck for support, he rubbed the head of his cock against my still-dripping hole and began to insert himself into my ass. I realised at once that he hadn't put any more lube on than what he got from me and that he didn't need any: I was wet and open from the three orgasms Chip had given me, warmed up and ready to be ridden hard. Randall slid in as if he were entering my pussy rather than my ass.

The movement forced the dildo higher up inside me, which in turn pushed my clit more firmly against it. Randall started moving inside me, thrusting slowly at first, building in speed and force, as I thrust back up to meet him. Chip grabbed a handful of my hair and pulled my head back, coming around to kiss me as deeply as Randall fucked me. I felt a peak building inside me, forcefully and powerfully, at a steady pace, until suddenly someone's hand came down on my ass check with a sting that made my climb to orgasm rush over me, a mad scramble up a steep ladder. The slap had been given by Randall, probably, but I was beyond being able to tell what belonged to who, and that thought pushed me all the way up and over the edge into another screaming orgasm so intense I felt like I was hovering between life and death. Chip moved his hand to that sweet spot between my pussy and my asshole, and stroked me furiously there, as Randall let out a bellow and quickened his pace, shouting as his orgasm shook him. I kept coming, every nerve in my body tautening and then releasing in long waves. Another groan joined our chorus, and I felt streams of Chip's hot come land on my ass, balancing the painting he'd given the front of me earlier.

I felt Randall go limp. He slid out of me and rolled off, as Chip let go and fell full-out onto the bed. Spent, slicked, satiated, I rolled into Chip while Randall snuggled against me. We slept as if we were three puppies.

I awoke in the morning to find myself sore, bruised and sticky. Not that I minded. I was still wearing the garter belt, but sometime in the night the stockings had come loose and were down at my ankles. I was alone in the bed. I could smell coffee brewing in the kitchen and heard Randall singing. When I called to him, he came in, holding a cup of steaming coffee. 'Found this in the bathroom,' he said, holding out a piece of paper. 'Lena and Randall,' it said, 'I had a great time. Thanks for inviting me into your fantasy, and I hope we get together again. Chip.' The note concluded with his phone number and email address. 'How about you?' Randall asked. 'Were you glad I invited Chip over?' He looked tender and concerned.

'Yeah,' I answered. 'Yeah.'

Randall stroked my hair affectionately. 'Me, too,' he said. Then he grinned mischievously and smacked my ass in a way as playful as last night's had been sexy. 'Good,' he said, 'now get into the shower. We're going to be late for breakfast. I made reservations. Dress slutty.'

My Delightful Torture
David Hawthorne

The day was warm so I wore only brief nylon running shorts from Pierre Cardin and Air Jordan tennis shoes. I decided to pick a trail that led into the centre of the forest. I estimated it would be about a six-mile run, there and back.

I jogged at a comfortable pace. I had worked up a light sweat and was really getting into the exercise.

Then I heard the screams.

I heard what sounded like sharp cries coming from off to my right. I slowed down, stopped. I heard it again, clearly:

'Don't, please! Stop!'

A female voice. Whoever she was, she was definitely in trouble. I walked, quietly as I could, in the direction where the pleas originated.

'Please, it hurts so much!'

166

I was off the trail, working my way through some fairly heavy undergrowth. The voice came again, and this time I heard another, also female: 'This is just the beginning, sweetie. Wait till you see what we've got planned for you next!' She was clearly enjoying whatever was happening.

I crouched and gazed through the bushes. There was an amazing scene to observe. It was a good-sized clearing. It was, or had been, some kind of camping/picnic area, because there were a couple of large, solid-looking picnic tables near the stream, and a stone fire ring that contained a small fire. What amazed me, though, were the occupants of the clearing. There were three young women there. One of them, the source of the cries for mercy, was hanging by her wrists from a tree limb and was being beaten by the other two. She had been tied so that her outstretched toes barely reached the ground, stretching her body for the whips that were being used by her attackers. She had a firm, slender body with slim hips and a taut ass, her breasts so small she was just about flat-chested; this was easy to see because she was completely naked, and her tormentors were dressed only in what appeared to be the bottom halves of the briefest thong bikinis I had ever seen in all my twenty-seven years.

I had an excellent view. The two aggressors, one a tall blonde and one a short redhead, both with decent C-cup tits, were using what appeared to be heavy five-tailed whips, with foot-and-a-half-long lashes. They were taking turns lashing the buttocks of their victim and they were enjoying the act; the strength of their blows, combined with the fact that their victim's buttocks showed no cuts, only redness, led me to conclude the whip tails must be made of some kind of rubber. I was sure that leather whips of such a size would have cut the girl to ribbons. Each time a blow landed on her tight, slender buttocks, her body jerked sharply.

My erection began to push against the interior of my running shorts. On my knees, peering through the brush, I pushed my shorts down to my thighs and began to stroke my cock clandestinely. I was so aroused it happened in two minutes: I ejaculated with three large spurts onto the twigs and dead leaves and dirt on the ground.

Then, behind me: 'Not bad.'

I jumped to my feet, prepared to run, but didn't when I was faced with a drop-dead gorgeous young lady in, I guessed, her early 20s. She was wearing the same pink thong as the two aggressors, but that was incidental to the two items she was carrying: in her right hand, a digital camcorder, which she held up to her eye and pointed straight at me; in her left, a .22 caliber Walther PPK, and it too was pointed straight at me. She was a tall girl, almost six feet, with the kind of athletic body I found easy to fantasise about worshipping. She had small, pointed breasts, a slim waist and long muscular legs. Her brunette hair was long and pulled into a ponytail that ended at her ass.

Standing in front of her with my shorts down around my legs and my cock still dripping semen made me feel dirty and perverted.

'Put your hands together on top of your head. I know how to use this gun and I will, if I have to.' She said this with a smile.

I did as told, lacing my fingers together and resting my hands on top of my skull.

'Can I pull my shorts up?' I asked her.

'You should be *ashamed* of yourself! What the hell are you doing here?'

'Just ... taking an afternoon jog.'

'You looked as if you were dreaming pretty well with that dick of yours in your hand,' she retorted. 'I've got a *great* video of you in action. Maybe you'd like a copy? I bet it would get a lot of hits on YouTube.' She lowered the battery-operated camera. The .22 pointed at my navel. She raised her voice: 'Ashleigh, you and the other girls get up here! Now! I got a little *surprise* for you.'

'Give me a break,' I pleaded softly. 'Let me pull up my shorts, at least.'

'You obviously *enjoyed* looking at my friends. I think it's only fair they get a good look at *you*, in return.'

The redhead was the first to arrive, followed by the two blondes. The blonde who had been the victim had put on a pink thong of her own and was the first to speak, with a southern accent.

'Who the heck is *this*? What the hay is he doin' here, Liza?'

'Just take it easy, Ashleigh,' said the gun-and-camera-toting Liza. 'He really *enjoyed* watching you being initiated. I've got the proof right here,' and she indicated the camcorder. 'He liked it so much he *jacked off*, right here, on *candid* camera. I just happened to discover the bloke being whacky.'

The blonde who had been doing the whipping moved close to me. She slowly looked me up and down, turned to the others and said in a thick Canadian accent, 'He's got a nice dick, eh? Nice body, too. Also kinda cute, eh.'

In spite of my fear, watching these four lovely women walk around in what amounted to g-strings was causing my penis to stir again.

'I think he likes us,' said the redhead, eying my cock that was now half-erect. 'What we gonna do wit' him?' She had a New York accent.

'Been thinking about that,' said Liza. 'How would you girls like to have some fun?'

They all nodded.

Liza said, 'Go on back to the camp. I'm going to explain the facts of life to the Yank. I'll fill you in shortly. Here, Ashleigh, take the camcorder with you.'

She gave the camera to the shorter blonde girl and the three went off, leaving me alone with Liza.

170

'Can I put down my hands and pull up my shorts?' I asked. 'You've still got the gun.'

She shrugged. 'Go ahead.'

I couldn't believe how comforting it was to pull my shorts back up over my genitals.

'What happens *now* is you have a choice to make.' She aimed the pistol steadily at my heart.

'What do you mean?'

She replied with a cute smile, 'I mean you can *choose* between my making sure that the tape I just shot of you jacking off in the woods finds its way "accidentally" to the coppers, or you can accept our punishment for your bad behaviour and I'll return the tape to you.'

The cops would never believe what they were doing in public and I would get into hot water for indecent exposure.

I inquired, 'What kind of punishment?'

'Let me explain. You have stumbled upon an initiation ceremony for a *very* exclusive girls' club. The cute blonde you saw being whipped is our newest member. Our club has no name and there are only the four of us. The club exists to allow us to explore our common interest in pain and pleasure. We are sadists, but our new members, as you witnessed with your Yankee peepers, must show they can *take* it before they can have the chance to dish it out. We normally play and experiment with one another – I'm the only member who has any experience playing with men. We use this campsite for our games because it's usually private, unless looky-loos like you happen by. Too bad for you, but wonderful for us, huh?'

'I ... I don't understand,' I said, although I had an idea of what she was getting at.

'You are going to let us *play* with you,' she said, 'if you don't want that tape to fall into the wrong hands.'

Nervously, I said, 'Define ..."play".'

'You will surrender yourself to us, here, tomorrow at noon. You will agree to accept any punishment we decide to implement for a period of four hours, an hour per girl. If you have taken all we can dish out, you'll be released and given the only copy of the tape.' Her eyes twinkled like she was talking about playing house with Barbie dolls.

'I can't agree to that,' I said. 'Four hours, you girls could do me some pretty serious damage.'

'We won't do anything that will do any horrid damage or leave any permanent evidence. That's always the way we play, and we're pretty good at it. Also, at any time, you can tell us you've had enough and we'll stop right away. If you do stop us, however, the tape gets to the coppers and online just as soon as I get to a laptop.'

'No damage to me then?' I couldn't believe I was calmly discussing this.

'Trust me,' she said, and giggled. 'If we *do* accidentally damage you, you can damage one of us. Not me – I never receive. I only give.'

I hesitated to seal the deal. 'Looks like I don't have much choice.'

'It will not be easy. This will be the *longest* four hours of your bloody life! But no blood,' and she giggled again.

I asked, 'What kind of clothes should I wear?'

'Anything you like. At high noon tomorrow, however, I want you standing in the centre of this little clearing, without a stitch of clothing. Is that perfectly clear?'

I cringed. 'Why do I have to be naked in front of you girls?'

'The nice thing about a naked man is that it's impossible for him to conceal his excitement.'

'Are you sure we can't just forget the whole thing?' I suggested. 'Blackmail me with money. I have five grand in the bank.'

She glared at me, serious. 'If you're not standing at attention, *in your birthday suit*, in the centre of this clearing tomorrow at noon, well ... you can imagine how it will go from there. Now, get the fuck out of here. I've got planning to do.'

I gladly left, running as fast as I could. I couldn't believe that I had agreed, very calmly, to present myself naked, at high noon, for four strange girls to torture me.

I dressed in running shorts and shoes, just as I had the day before; you can say I was dressed for whatever delightful torture awaited. It was 11.35 when I parked,

173

and I took my time getting to the clearing. I looked around and saw no one. I removed my running shoes, then my nylon shorts, and moved through the undergrowth to the clearing. Once in the centre, I stood at attention as instructed, feeling foolish.

They appeared from the direction of the campsite. They all wore white leather thongs and high-heeled black leather boots. Their breasts were bare. They were well dressed for the occasion as well.

Liza was the first to speak. 'You are wondering why we are dressed as we are. Simply to add to your torment. I know you find our bodies attractive and I also know that a stiff cock is a lot more susceptible to torment than a soft one. Of course, I assume you'll try to avoid becoming sexually aroused, but with us dressed like this I imagine you'll have a fairly difficult time.'

I asked, 'Do you just want to humiliate me?'

'It goes much *deeper* than that, mister.' She reached down and gave my cock a couple of smooth strokes. When it noticeably stiffened, Liza flashed an evil grin and I heard one of the other girls giggle. She gave me a nudge in the general direction of the campsite and we started walking towards it. Once there, I realised that this was almost surely going to be much worse than I had thought. There were picnic tables and one had been covered with an old blanket.

The blonde victim from yesterday, Ashleigh, came

forward with a thick nylon rope in her hand, pushing her flat chest out, the nipples hard and erect. She tied my wrists together and tossed the end of the rope over a thick tree branch that was about nine feet off the ground. One of the other girls took the end and drew me up to my fullest stretch, still allowing me to touch the ground with my feet, before tying the rope off on a lower branch. I was strung up by my wrists but able to stand comfortably. Then they quickly drove heavy metal stakes into the ground at my feet, about four feet apart.

Watching these lovely girls work, the thongs disappearing between firm, tanned buttocks, their young breasts gleaming with a soft sheen of perspiration, caused my cock to behave as though I was actually looking forward to the coming event.

Once the stakes were in place, my ankles were tied to them with more lengths of the thick rope, stretching my legs apart and leaving me almost suspended by my wrists above my head. My ankles were pulled out to a point where I was just barely able to maintain contact with the ground with the tips of my toes. The position was not comfortable.

Liza walked around me, making sure everything was snug. She asked if I was comfortable. I didn't respond. She took hold of my cock, which was growing larger, and began to stroke it. Her stroking was gentle, but it contained a firmness of grip that told me she knew exactly what she was doing. Of course my cock responded to her manipulation. Once it was fully erect, she abandoned it and began to work on my nipples. She teased them with her fingernails, then, pinching savagely, let me know how easy it was for her to hurt me. My cry of pain pleased her and she released the tender nubs while she looked me directly in the eyes and spoke.

'Now,' she said seriously, 'the *first* thing we're going to do is see how far we can stretch your balls.'

She brought forward a four-foot length of thin nylon clothesline, halved it, then made a loop at its centre by pulling the loose ends back through. She placed the loop around the base of my scrotum, above the balls and below the penis, and pulled it snug. Then she took the loose ends, threaded them through the loop and between my balls so as to separate them, and pulled the ends tight. She gave the ends a firm tug, demonstrating that pulling on them created more pressure, and, of course, *pain*.

'Those poor little things are starting to get a little purple already,' cooed Liza. I could tell this was turning her on, and I was certain I could smell her pussy getting wet.

The taller blonde produced a yellow plastic pail from under one of the picnic tables and tied the handle to the loose ends of the clothesline that separated my balls, allowing the pail to hang free about eight inches above the ground. The pail didn't weigh much, but knowing that things could easily be put into the pail to make it heavier had me nervously anticipating their next action.

My cock was still semi-erect in spite of my fear, or, perhaps, because of it …

'How much weight do you think your family jewels can support?' Ashleigh asked with a serious tone of curiosity.

'Water is reasonably heavy, so let's just find out,' said Liza. 'Girls, let's have some H_2O, shall we?'

While Ashleigh went to get a plastic gallon water jug that had been on the covered picnic table, the other three amused themselves playing with my naked body. The redhead pinched my nipples and ran her hand lightly up and down my chest and belly; the other blonde slapped my buttocks for firmness; Liza held my cock in her left hand and, looking directly into my eyes, scraped a sharp fingernail over its sensitive head. The combination of stimulation and pain was quite overwhelming.

Ashleigh joined them, holding the gallon jug.

'A gallon of water weighs about six pounds,' Liza said. 'That bucket suspended from your balls will hold two gallons. I'm not sure you can take twelve pounds tied to your balls. That's a *lot* of weight to suspend from those tender little baby-batter makers. What do you think?'

I wasn't given a chance to reply. Ashleigh tilted her pail over the one hanging from my balls and let the water begin to fill it. The increased weight was immediately uncomfortable. I began to feel a dull ache deep in my testicles. She stopped after putting about a half-gallon in my pail and they all watched my reactions as the pail swung tautly between my legs. At a signal from Liza, Ashleigh poured the rest. I could feel the rope separating my balls tighten from the additional weight.

'How does it *feel* now?' Liza raised a perfectly formed bare foot and gave the pail a little nudge with her toes, causing it to swing forwards and back between my legs in a gentle arc. Each swing seemed to tighten the rope a bit more, causing my cock to bob around like it had a mind of its own.

'I don't think I can take any more!' I cried. '*Please*. Get that thing off me before I suffer serious damage! I'd like to have children someday!'

'Don't be such a *bitch*,' Liza said, her voice harsh. 'I'm sure a fine physical specimen such as yourself can handle more than a *mere* six pounds. I believe we need some more water.'

Ashleigh went to get a second jug.

Liza roughly grabbed my cock. 'I *told* you we wouldn't do any permanent damage, didn't I? Don't you *trust* me?'

I decided to remain quiet, hoping that she really knew what she was doing.

Ashleigh returned quickly. She looked at Liza expectantly and, receiving a nod, began to pour more water into the pail, stopping only when things reached the point where I was certain my testicles were about to burst or, even worse, be torn from my flesh.

Liza examined the pail and strummed the taut clothes-line several times, like a harp string. It was causing me sheer agony.

'That's about ten pounds,' she said. 'I guess that's about all he can take, girls. Let's see how he handles *that* for a while.'

They gathered around me and amused themselves by teasing and tormenting me with their hands. I was unable to resist reacting to their fingers digging into my sides; they were delighted at my ticklishness. Each sudden movement, of course, led to immediate pain in my tethered balls.

I groaned for mercy between ticklish laughs.

Liza said, 'Girls, let's give him a little rest, now. We don't want to *break* our toy before we've had our fun.'

She lifted the pail and poured its heavy contents onto the ground. My relief was immediate, though I suspected the dull ache in my balls would not subside for some time.

They gathered around again.

'He's got a very nice body,' said one of my tormenters.

Liza replied, 'Wait until he feels *the clips*!'

One of the other girls mumbled something about enjoying the sight of my cock swinging in the breeze.

'I think it's time to see how he likes our *little whips*,' Liza announced.

They released me and allowed me to rest a few minutes on the ground, at their leather-booted feet, while they removed the stakes and put the ropes away.

Liza ordered me to my feet. She held a pair of red handcuffs. She cuffed my wrists together in front of me. The cuffs fitted snugly but not tightly enough to pinch my skin. Next, a pair of sturdy thumbcuffs was produced by the redhead and placed on my big toes, locking my feet close together. Liza took a very long piece of thin nylon clothesline and doubled it at the midpoint. She placed the loose ends of the line through the midpoint loop, around my waist, drawing it uncomfortably tight, with the loose ends hanging down from near my navel. She then brought the free ends down my lower belly to my genitals and drew them back between my legs, passing one loose end around either side of my genitals. The ends of the line came back together behind my balls, nesting snugly in the crack of my ass. They were then drawn up behind me and, at the small of my back, passed through the loop around my waist.

Liza then directed me to raise my handcuffed wrists above my head. When I complied, she passed the ends under the short chain connecting the cuffs, then drew them over the same tree limb above my head. When the girls began pulling the line over the limb, my hands were drawn up over my head and the thin rope dug deeply, and painfully, into the cleft between my buttocks. They drew it up until I was on tiptoes, with the thumbcuffs preventing me from any kicking about or other unusual leg movement. The line felt like it was cutting me in half between my legs; it was supporting almost my entire weight.

They finally tied the line off so I was just able to reach the ground with my toes, but I was unable to make any movement without causing myself intense pain.

They all gathered closely around me, enjoying my reaction to this very creative bondage. Once again, in spite of my fear, my cock was growing erect. I tried to grasp the line above my head with my cuffed hands, hoping to take some of my weight off it between my legs, but it was too thin for me to gain any benefit. My hands simply slipped off its surface.

'Get the whips!' Liza commanded.

'The whips' turned out to be four little brown leather riding crops; each girl grasped one and began taking turns slashing at my naked body. I was unable to move around very much because of the line drawn up into my ass, and it was quite painful. All I could do was dangle there in front of them and take it. The crops were thin enough that they didn't break my skin but they smarted like scorpion stings. The girls concentrated their blows on my buttocks and thighs. The combination of the savage little whips and the line had me in a fog-like daze of pain and pleasure.

Liza ordered the others to stop and she dug into the box and brought out wooden clothes-pegs. She showed them to me for a moment, and began placing them on my cock. 'You'll appreciate this,' she said. 'They hurt when they go on, but they hurt a lot *worse* when they come off.' She put several of them on both sides of my cock, and several more on my sensitive tip. They hurt, all right; when she began flicking them with her forefinger they felt like wasp stings.

The girls were fascinated by the sight of the clothes-pegs dangling from my erect dick.

Liza said, 'OK, bitches, listen: why don't you use those nifty crops to take those clothes-pegs off?'

They were delighted by the suggestion, or order. They whipped my cock, and I almost lost it. They slashed at the clothes-pegs like cats in heat, trying to make them disconnect from my swollen, tender manhood. Every move I made to try to avoid the pain caused the thin nylon line to cut deeper into my crotch. Ashleigh was particularly rambunctious, pinching my nipples with one hand while pumping away at my tortured cock with the other. They released me from the line between my legs, removed the handcuffs from my wrists and the thumb-cuffs from my toes, and allowed me another brief rest. I was relieved, and a little surprised, to discover no blood running down my legs.

They led me over to one of the sturdy picnic tables.

It was the one that had been covered with a blanket, to prevent splinters, I guessed, but I wasn't given much time to contemplate that fact. I quickly found myself bound spread-eagled to the four corners of the table. I was face up and stretched as tightly as they could manage. I was beginning to wonder if I wouldn't have been better off to let them do whatever they wanted with the videotape. My continuing, and very visible, sexual excitement, however, made me realise I was just kidding myself. I would let them do almost anything to me, if only they would give me an orgasm or two.

'It's time for you to feel a little *heat*,' Liza said, casually stroking my cock. 'First, we're going to apply a little bit of hot candle wax to some of your more sensitive places ... then we're gonna take it off. Sounds like *fun*, huh? First, though, we've got to try to make sure your cock stays as hard as possible for this procedure. This ought to help.'

She produced a short length of the thin line, tied it tightly around the base of my genitals and then used the ends to wrap around and tightly separate my balls before tying them off.

'There. Things ought to stay pretty tight and firm with that. Your balls are getting purple, again. Does *this* hurt?'

'This' was a sharp fingernail, digging into my taut left testicle. My gasp of pain gave her the answer she wanted. She brought out and lit a white candle that appeared to

183

be about a half-inch thick and about eight inches long. She carefully began to drip the burning wax from the candle onto my nipples. It was very hot, and she was holding the candle only about two inches above my chest as she dripped the wax.

Coating my nipples with wax was to be the least of it. After my nipples were generously covered, she began to slowly cover the shaft of my cock. This was very painful, particularly because she was holding the candle so close to my flesh. The other girls were watching my reactions closely and they seemed almost stunned by the violence of my struggles against my bonds.

Liza began to drip the burning wax slowly onto the head of my cock. The line around the base of my cock kept me erect, but I wasn't sure I could handle much more of this. Hot wax from two inches above the most sensitive part of an erect penis is very scary stuff. Each drip felt like a hot needle through my flesh.

When she finished covering the head of my cock and began to drip the wax on my tightly tied balls, I yelled aloud, much to the delight of my audience. The scrotal sac is covered with very thin skin. I was sure I was being blistered with each and every drip of wax.

She finished her painful work, leaving me trembling with relief, my nipples and genitals completely covered with the now hard wax.

'Here's your big chance,' Liza said. 'We've got to take

this wax off you, so we might as well have some fun in the process. Each of us is going to take off our thong and crawl up there on top of you. You are going to try to bring us to an orgasm. We'll be facing your cock, with our sweet little pussies right over your mouth. You'll be able to reach our clits with your tongue, if you try real hard. Make each one of us come with your tongue, and the rest of this session will be very easy for you. Oh, I forgot to mention that, while you are trying to get us off with your tongue, we'll be removing the wax from your cock and balls with this ...'

She had an automotive test probe, about six inches long, that looked like a screwdriver but had a very sharp point. The sharp point, she explained matter-of-factly, was ideal for removing hard wax from sensitive places, a fact she demonstrated by carefully removing the wax from my nipples. It hurt a great deal. Each small piece of wax she flicked away required her to dig the sharp point of the probe into the tender skin beneath the wax. I could only imagine how bad it would be when they started working on my cock and balls ...

Liza was the first to mount me. She removed her thong and positioned herself with her knees on either side of my chest, facing my genitals, so that, as promised, I could reach up with my straining tongue and stimulate her clitoris. She tasted sweet and warm, and her body reacted immediately to my efforts. Torturing me must have really turned her on. She tried to resist her reactions by digging sharply into my cock and tightly stretched balls with the probe, and she did slow me down somewhat. In less than five minutes, however, she came vigorously, with loud shuddering sobs. The watching girls were hushed as she finished and I hoped my excellent efforts might have earned me a reprieve. They recovered quickly, however, and argued briefly about whose turn it was to go next.

Each of them, in turn, climbed on the table and presented me with a soft warm pussy. I was able to lick and suck their clits and, yes, brought each of them to a climax, but, while I was doing that, they used the sharp screwdriver probe to remove every speck of the wax from my cock and balls. I tried to maintain my concentration, but the pain of having a sharp instrument digging into the head of my cock was more than I could bear. After what seemed an eternity of agony, the last of them was spent and my cock and balls were clean of the wax.

In spite of all the things that had been done to me, I was still enchanted by Liza. She was breathtakingly beautiful, with a demeanour that made me sexually excited just from being in her presence.

'You've shown you can take a lot,' she whispered into my ear. 'We're going to make you come now. Are you ready for that?'

'Yes,' I said.

'You *may* regret that.'

'I don't care,' and at that point this was the truth.

'You heard him, girls. Let's get him off.'

She untied the line around my cock and balls and discarded it, then produced a bag full of white plastic clothes-pegs. They were the type that had serrations in the pinching ends to create a positive grip, a fact she pointed out by placing one in front of my concerned eyes and opening and closing it slowly. She began carefully placing them around the ridge on the head of my cock. Each of them created its own special kind of pain as it was applied. When she was done, there were ten of them, tightly gripping the ridge. She gave my cock a mild shaking, causing the pegs to bounce around merrily. The pain was exquisite.

'This is your "reward" for being such a good victim,' she said, taking a firm grip on my cock's shaft. I was still spread-eagled to the table, helpless to prevent anything she wished to do. She began to stroke my cock firmly, causing me to gasp aloud at the renewed pain caused by the moving clothes-pegs.

'I know you think this is very bad now, but you won't believe *how* bad it is when you start to come.'

I wasn't sure what she meant. Her soft hand on my sensitised shaft was rapidly bringing me to the point of no return, in spite of the agony the clothes-pegs were causing. Watching my eyes carefully, she increased the tempo of her strokes as I neared my plateau, every stroke jiggling the clothes-pegs and causing me excruciating pain.

'When you come,' Liza said, slowing her stroke slightly to drop me back before the final blast, 'you aren't going to believe how painful it is. Every ejaculatory surge will cause the head of your cock to expand. Unfortunately for you, these clips around the head of your cock don't have any room to expand. They're inclined to just sort of hang around and bite in. The result is excruciating pain. Each time your cock surges to ejaculate, the pins will bite in even tighter than they feel now. It's the perfect combination of pain and pleasure. You won't be able to avoid the pain, and you won't be able to resist the pleasure. All we need to make this perfect is a couple of nasty little clamps for your nipples.'

Such words from the mouth of so very young a girl.

Ashleigh produced a couple of very severe-looking alligator clamps. She carefully prepared my nipples for them, pulling and tugging until they were ready, then placed them expertly on the very tips of my nipples. They hurt terribly.'Here we *go*,' Liza said, squeezing my cock.

I couldn't resist. She took me rapidly to the point of no return then, smiling sadistically, finished the job. I came. Each surge, as promised, was excruciatingly painful. The head of my cock tried to expand and there was no place to go. The pain was like ten red-hot needles through my dick. Yet, at the same time, I was feeling an ecstasy like I had never experienced before. Pain and pleasure made an explosive mixture and I came in rivers ...

Liza took the clothes-pegs off my cock, one at a time. Each left its mark of agonising shame. When they were all gone, I was totally spent.

'Guess what?' Liza said.

I was still dazed.

'It's after five. Your ordeal is over,' she said. 'Girls, would you leave us alone, please?'

The other girls left the clearing. I was still tied to the picnic table, but as soon as they were out of sight she released me.

'Where's my copy of the videotape?' I asked.

'Here.' She placed it on the table. 'I do have one confession to make,' she said. 'I made one extra copy. To be safe.'

I smiled. 'You're a cunning little bitch.'

'Yeah,' with a smirk, 'but you can't deny you *liked* what we did to you, in spite of the pain. A stiff cock tells no lies.'

'What do I have to do to get the copy?'

She glared. 'Be here next Saturday, *naked*. I'll be alone. It'll just be you and me. Dressed for it.'

The thought of being at lovely Liza's mercy again, and of what she would be wearing, caused a rush of perverted excitement to run from my head to my cock.

'If you hadn't asked me,' I started to say ...
'Oh,' she said, looking at my new erection, '*I know.*'